"I promise you if you let me go,
I shall not mention this to anyone,"
Harriet stammered in fright.

"Promises are easily broken that are given without any token. What 'ud you say if'n I asked for one?"

"What sort of token?" Harriet asked in bewilderment. "I have no money nor any jewels. My word should be enough."

His harsh laughter mocked her. "Any doings between a man and a maid are settled with something a little warmer than words. If you won't give me a token of your own free will, I shall have to take one for myself, either that or silence you in some other fashion!"

One muscular arm grasped Harriet's slender waist, firm fingers forcing her chin upwards so that indignant brown eyes glared fulminatingly into gray.

"Release me instantly!" Harriet commanded breathlessly.

"Not until I have my token!" the smuggler replied.

"Very well," Harriet cried, when she saw there was no escape. "Take your token, but it is my word that binds me to my promise," she told him proudly, "and not something you wrest from me by force of arms."

"Pride is a good thing in a victor, Missie," the smuggler replied hardily, "but it makes a uncomfortable bed for the vanquished."

The smuggler's lips crushed Harriet's furious response. Her mouth stinging and her heart pounding, Harriet found herself set free . . .

Novels By Caroline Courtney

Duchess in Disguise
A Wager For Love
Love Unmasked
Guardian of The Heart
Dangerous Engagement
Love's Masquerade
Love Triumphant

Published By
WARNER BOOKS

CAROLINE COURTNEY

Love Triumphant

WARNER BOOKS

A Warner Communications Company

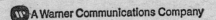

chapter one

"Oh, no! It would be misty, tonight of all nights. Now I shall be really late!"

Tightening her hold on Betsy's reins, Harriet glanced apprehensively over her shoulder. She was not normally given to speaking her thoughts out loud, but there was something about this particular stretch of land, after dark, that made her long for the reassurance of a human voice, even if it was only her own.

As she had suspected, the mist was rolling in fast. Already the mouth of the estuary had been blotted out by the creeping wall of whiteness. She suppressed her growing agitation and concentrated on encouraging Betsy to increase her normal walking pace to something approaching a trot. Poor Betsy, she thought fondly. She had been pulling the vicarage pony trap forever and was inclined to take her own time, ignoring her young mistress's anxious commands to move a little faster.

It was as well that she was so familiar with the road, Harriet reflected, otherwise she might have found herself in very dire straits indeed! The mist had obliterated the estuary now, only the odd clump of trees emerging from the gloom to serve as landmarks as she urged Betsy homeward.

The day had been cold, and evening had brought frost crackling through the rushes, stiff as soldiers at the water's edge. Betsy shied at a rabbit bemused by the mist. Harriet frowned. They would be growing anxious at the vicarage. Old Granny Hopkins, at the farm, had kept her chattering long after her errand had been completed, pressing cake and milk on her young guest and plainly glad of an opportunity to indulge in a little feminine gossip.

Despite his own aristocratic connections, her papa took his duties as Vicar very seriously indeed. Harriet had helped her mama with the sick-visiting in the parish almost as soon as she could walk. Not that Granny Hopkins had been sick, but she had been glad enough of Mama's elderberry wine and the recipe she had promised to aid young Peter's cough.

The road dipped and narrowed, a thick gray blanket pressing itself wetly around Harriet and the trap. Betsy stood still and refused to move. Sighing, Harriet climbed down to see what was amiss.

It was March, but it was as cold as midwinter, the ground still in the iron grip of frost and the murky hours of daylight quickly gone. Harriet's Papa shook his head and told his ladies that the *Morning Post* reported that the Thames had practically frozen over!

Betsy rolled her eyes at Harriet's approach. The pony was a dear, but willfully stubborn, with a mind of her own, and plainly she did not wish to move. Papa said that on a Vicar's stipend they could not possibly afford to keep a carriage and pair, as they did up at the Hall. Harriet repressed a small sigh. Papa decried such worldly considerations as wealth and position as being unworthy of a member of the clergy, but Harriet's turbulent spirit rebelled. It seemed so unfair that Mama was forced to endure the slights and petty insults of her sister-in-law, and all because she had married a younger son! Not that Papa was just anyone's younger son. Although Mama had cautioned Harriet never to boast of the fact, Papa was, after all, the grandson of an Earl!

Harriet wished that Betsy had chosen to stop anywhere other than Smugglers' Wood, as this part of the estuary was known locally. By rights the wood belonged to Sir Peter Dale, now long dead. With his demise the estate had fallen into disrepair, the sea reclaiming the marshes and creeping insiduously inland. There were strange rumors concerning Smugglers Wood, garbled tales of mysterious headless figures, and ghostly horses, moving silent as the grave and leaving no trace to show where they had been.

Harriet and her cousins, Sophy and Philip, had shivered in terrified delight when the ser-

7

vants talked about the wood, until Philip outgrew such childish occupations and told his sister and cousin with scornful masculine superiority that the "phantoms" were really smugglers, who made good use of the wood's sinister reputation by using it as an overland route for their contraband cargoes.

Harriet had been inclined to dispute Philip's claims until her papa confirmed them. Not that he would ever condone the free-trading—far from it—nor would he accept the brandy and wine that appeared so mysteriously in the vicarage stables. He, he told his wife and daughter sternly, would never consecrate a service in stolen wine! Mama's brother, Sir George Wyclyffe, was less nice and often told his brother-in-law in hearty tones that he was a fool not to accept what was offered and no one a penny the wiser. *He* found it hard enough to make ends meet with a growing son and two daughters to provide for, and heaven knows, he could account himself a wealthy man indeed compared with poor Gerald! How on earth he managed to contrive so well with only his living and the small allowance he received from the present Earl, Sir George did not know!

Bitterly regretting that she had taken the shorter road in order to avoid being too late for supper, Harriet lifted Betsy's hooves, one by one, to make sure that there were no stones lodging in them which might have been hurting the pony. She was just inspecting the last one, crouched on the ground, her cloak damp from its contact with the frost-rimed earth, when she heard the faint but unmistakable sounds of horses' hooves. Petrified, Harriet froze, too terrified to make any attempt to conceal her presence. An eerily silent string of horses swayed slowly past, shrouded by the mist. A rider checked and stared in Harriet's direction.

Detaching himself from the column, the man rode toward her. Harriet could see that the other horses carried barrels strapped on either side of their backs, or huge flat oblong packs. It was the smugglers Philip had told them about. The oblong parcels would be the smuggled silks that fetched such high prices in London, and the barrels the wines and brandies. She closed her eyes, still crouched at Betsy's feet, trembling from top to toe.

Papa had told her that spirits and silks were not the only things the smugglers brought from France. There were more sinister articles that entered and left the country in this fashion. Letters to Bonaparte's many spies, gathering the information that the Frenchman hoped would one day enable him to invade the English coast. Papa's voice grew very serious when he talked of these spies. Only last week he had read out to Harriet an article in the *Morning Post* deploring the lax security arrangements operating in some military circles. Because he had not had a son, Papa had tended to treat Harriet very much as though *she* were a boy, and hence her understanding of such subjects as Greek and Latin was far in advance of that of any other young lady of her upbringing—and a good many young men! Harriet had been encouraged to make free of her father's modest library, and while other young ladies were sighing over the mysteries of

Udolpho and Lord Byron's burning lines, she had been studying Plato and the other Greek classics.

Horse and rider stopped. Risking a terrified upward glance, Harriet saw that the file of horses had disappeared; there was only the solitary rider, motionless above her.

He was wearing a tattered frieze coat, filthy and torn, a soiled woollen muffler obscuring the lower half of his face, but it was his eyes that held Harriet's attention. They were dark gray, the same color as the mist eddying about them. His hair was damp, where it had escaped from his greasy sailor's cap; it was black, she noticed, and very thick.

For a common smuggler he had an unwarranted air of assurance. Harriet trembled under his scrutiny, wondering if her last hour had come, and prayed that somehow she might wake to find herself safe and warm at home in her own bed.

"Spying on us, was you?" he asked as he swung down from his horse. Somehow hearing the familiar country accent lent Harriet courage.

Straightening up, she tilted her chin firmly and replied, "Certainly not! My pony stumbled in the mist."

Before she could stop him, he was down on his knees running his hands over Betsy's legs.

"Seems all right to me," he grunted suspiciously. "What be you a-doing here anyways? Don't you know these parts ain't reckoned to be safe after dark?"

"I was on my way home," Harriet retorted stiffly, not liking his familiarity. "I was visiting

Granny Hopkins and hadn't realized how late it was."

She knew she was gabbling like an idiot, but the relief at finding herself still alive was making her almost light-headed.

The smuggler's eyes narrowed.

"Granny Hopkins, was it, eh? A strange place for the likes of you, missie, b'ain't it?"

Before Harriet could stop him, his calloused hands were touching the stuff of her pelisse. She shuddered, pulling back, and saw his expression harden as he stared down into her heart-shaped face.

"B'ain't worrying, be you, missie?" he jeered softly. "What be your business with Granny Hopkins, anyways? Related to her, are you?"

"My papa is the Vicar," Harriet replied stiffly.

The smuggler's face twisted sardonically. "Oh, playing the grand lady, was you? More fool you, to come home through these woods. Don't you know how the 'brotherhood' treat spies?"

"I wasn't spying," Harriet reiterated, almost stammering with fright. "I promise you if you let me go, I shall not mention this to anyone!"

"How can I believe the promise of the loikes of you?" the smuggler taunted. "A fine lady loike you will waste no time in setting the militia upon us!"

He saw that Harriet was staring into his face and laughed harshly. "Know me again, will you, missie? Trying to decide how you'll describe me to the magistrates, are you? Thinking of the day when you will see me swinging from a gibbet?"

"Oh, no!" Harriet exclaimed in shocked accents. "If you will just go away, I promise you I shall say *nothing!*"

She shivered again at the expression in his eyes. Such very strange eyes, different from any she had ever seen before. She much preferred a man to have blue eyes like her cousin Philip's, Harriet thought suddenly, or brown like Papa's.

"Promises are easily broken that are given without any token. What 'ud you say if'n I asked for one?"

"What sort of token?" Harriet asked in bewilderment. "I have no money, nor any jewels . . . I . . ."

"There's other things," the smuggler suggested softly. "Things that 'ud mean a lot more to a girl like you!"

"I shall give you my word," Harriet told him stiffly, alarm feathering along her spine. "If you will not accept that, there is nothing else."

His harsh laughter mocked her.

"Your word! We may be rough and ready where I comes from, but any doings between a man and a maid are settled with something a little warmer than words!"

Harriet's brown eyes sparkled indignantly. She tossed her sable ringlets and drew herself up to her full five feet two inches. "If you are implying that you expect *me* to indulge in the same free and easy manners as your *friends,* sir, you are greatly at outs!" she announced darkly, grasping Betsy's reins.

The smuggler's laugh died. His eyes grew cold, and he eyed Harriet with contempt.

"Be that so! Well then, missie, if you won't give me a token of your own free will, I shall have to take one for myself, either that or silence you in some other fashion!"

One muscular arm grasped Harriet's slender waist, firm fingers forcing her chin upward so that indignant brown eyes glared fulminatingly into gray.

"Release me instanter!" Harriet commanded breathlessly.

"Not until I have my token!" the smuggler replied.

His shirt was unlaced, and her small pummelling fists beat wildly at the smooth, damp skin. It was all to no avail. The smuggler held her as easily as he might have done a child, laughing at her vain attempts to free herself.

"Very well," Harriet cried, when she saw there was no escape. "Take your token, but it is my word that binds me to my promise," she told him proudly, "and not something you wrest from me by force of arms."

"Pride is a good thing in a victor, missie," the smuggler replied hardily, "but it makes an uncomfortable bed for the vanquished."

The smuggler's lips crushed Harriet's furious response, exacting full payment for her earlier defiance. Her mouth stinging and her heart beating like a drum, Harriet found herself set free, while the smuggler watched her color come and go with callous indifference. "Now, I shall accept your promise not to speak of this night's doings. Be thankful that I was the only one to see you, missie. My companions might not have been disposed to be so lenient!"

"Lenient!" Is that what you call it?" Involuntarily Harriet's fingers trembled against her bruised lip. Tears were not very far away, and her legs were threatening to give way under her.

"Perhaps I am a fool after all," the smuggler said as he stared arrogantly at Harriet. "Any man is, who accepts a woman's word."

Hot words of denial leaped to Harriet's lips, but were quickly suppressed. Papa had taught her the importance of keeping one's promises, however unwillingly given! She returned the smuggler's stare.

"Perhaps you do not know the right women, sir!" she riposted coolly.

The smuggler was unimpressed.

"Right, wrong—what does it matter? All cats are gray at night, child, or haven't you learned that yet?" He looked a little more closely at her. "No, of course you haven't," he said a shade bitterly. "A girl like you, protected, cossetted, wrapped in warm cloaks . . ."

His words stirred Harriet to unwilling pity. She was her father's daughter and knew how the poor fisherfolk lived. It would do no good at all to point out to this man that she was as despised by her peers as the smuggler seemed to think he was by her. The pelisse she was wearing was one of cousin Sophy's cast-offs, a thick, warm wool, but of last year's color, or so Sophy had gaily assured her.

Betsy moved restlessly as though anxious to be gone. The smuggler stepped backwards and remounted.

"A word to the wise, missie. If you play me false, I shall know of it, and it will be the worse for you, and not just you," he told her grimly. "You love your father, don't you?"

Harriet clutched the side of the trap nervously. The smuggler smiled mirthlessly.

"To our next meeting, missie!" He doffed his greasy cap, not seeming to notice the cold, nor the rents in his inadequate coat, so different from Harriet's warm pelisse.

She got into the trap without looking at him, turning only once to stare at the space where he had been, now empty and silent, so that she could almost suppose the whole incident to have been no more than a dream.

An hour later, comfortably ensconced before the parlor fire, Harriet was inclined to believe that it had been. At least she would have been, were her lips not still tender from the smuggler's ruthless assault. *That* had not been a dream. A nightmare, rather!

Elizabeth Willoughby eyed her daughter anxiously. She had been on the point of imploring her husband to send a messenger to her brother to say that Harriet had not returned home, when Betsy had trotted up the drive. The culprit had received an admonishing lecture from her papa and an injunction to make sure she set out for home earlier on another occasion, before tucking into a bowl of Mama's homemade soup. For such a tiny, elfin figure she had an extremely large appetite, Papa teased, and it was true that Harriet was only slightly built, with fragile bones and features that owed their attractiveness more to a bewitchingly animated countenance than to any classical beauty.

Harriet's large brown eyes grew somber as she stared into the fire. Philip would be home

15

by now. Up at the Hall they would be dining in much more style than they adopted at the vicarage. Sir George made no bones about the fact that he considered his pretty sister had wasted herself on a mere clergyman in holy orders, no matter who his grandfather might have been and his wife tended to sniff disparagingly whenever Harriet's parents were mentioned, telling her cronies that dearest Elizabeth had married "for love" and for that reason she was not too anxious for *her* daughters to spend too much time in their aunt's company. They, like their mama, would marry where their parents chose, sensible, prestigious marriages that would add to their mama's consequence!

Harriet was well aware of her aunt's intentions. She and Sophy were much of an age, and Sophy, a lively chatterbox of a blonde, was inclined to confide artlessly in her cousin without considering that some of her mama's more astringent comments might prove hurtful to the daughter of the man she affected to despise.

"Of course, what really infuriates Mama is that your father makes not the slightest push to bring himself to the attention of his grand relations," Philip had told Harriet the last time he was home, and Harriet was very much afraid he was right.

Dearest Philip! He was four and twenty to her nineteen, and she had worshipped him as a child, following doggedly in his wake unaware that her childish adoration was blossoming into a different sort of love. He had seemed like a god to her dazzled adolescent eyes, returning from Oxford laden with comfits for his sisters and

Harriet, teasing and lordly in his assumption that they were all ready to hang on his every word.

Harriet's color deepened in a fashion that had nothing to do with the heat of the fire. Until recently she had never dared to suppose that Philip felt anything but cousinly affection for her, but even Sophy had commented on the very pointed manner in which he had stared at her when he said goodbye at Christmas. Until that moment, Harriet doubted that he had ever seen her as anything other than a tiresome child, but it had been six months since he last saw her—six months during which she had matured from girl to woman, and the frank admiration in Philip's eyes told her that he was at last aware of that fact.

From that moment a tremulous happiness had grown within her, hope alternating with despair as she counted the days until his next visit. Now he was home once more. She smiled dreamily, the smuggler forgotten. What would he say to her when they met? Would his eyes widen in appreciation? Would he be distant and adult, or would he treat her as he had always done, giving her a bear hug and a light peck on the cheek?

"Harriet, my love, you are all but asleep! Bed at once!"

"Yes, Mama." She made no attempt to resist her mama's commands. Truth to tell, she *was* tired, and besides, she would have the whole night to dream of Philip! Her toes curled with delicious anticipation. Elizabeth Willoughby frowned and placed a hand against her daughter's alabaster forehead.

"Oh, dear, I do hope you aren't starting with a chill, Harriet, you look quite flushed!"

"It's only the heat of the fire, Mama."

She kissed her mother's cheek and dropped her father a demure curtsy, stifling a yawn as she walked upstairs. At the Hall they would be sitting in the drawing room now. Young Lucy would have been banished to her bedroom, but Sophy would still be up, perhaps singing a duet with Philip whilst her mama looked on critically. Harriet stifled a tiny sigh.

Contrary to Elizabeth Willoughby's fears, Harriet did not go down with a chill, but her mama insisted that she stay within doors for two days following her adventure lest some capricious ailment be lurking outside waiting to pounce on her unwary daughter. Harriet laughed at her mama's fears.

"I may look frail, Mama, but you know I am as strong as a horse!"

"Even horses need warm stables," Elizabeth Willoughby commented waspishly. "You still look very pale, Harriet. I have persuaded your father that you must stay at home, at least for a week, although, of course, you cannot miss church on Sunday."

Unhappily for Elizabeth Willoughby's plans, the next day brought an urgent missive from the Hall, begging Harriet to take pity on her cousin, who was about to die from sheer boredom, by calling to visit her.

Nothing loath, Harriet informed her mama that a brisk walk was just what she needed after three days cooped up in the narrow confines of the vicarage.

Following the death of the old Vicar, Sir George had lost no time in offering the living, which was within his gift, to his brother-in-law, excusing his generosity by saying that he missed his sister and would welcome having her and her family living so close to the Hall.

That had been before Harriet's birth, when her parents had been living in a tiny parish just outside London, and so she had never known anywhere but the Marsh.

The vicarage was some two miles from the Hall if one went by road, using the impressive gravel drive that swept through an avenue of elms, but there was a well-worn path used by the younger members of the respective households. It skirted the vicarage lawn, cutting across a field and through the Hall's shrubberies; and within half an hour of leaving the vicarage, Harriet was tripping up to the door of the Hall.

chapter two

To Harriet's dismay a footman informed her
that Sophy was in the small drawing room with
her mama. Sophy was seated in an uncomfortable hard-backed chair designed to improve any
reluctant young lady's posture, her fair head
obediently bent over her embroidery, while Lady
Phoebe worked at her tambour frame, her eagle
eye on her eldest daughter to ensure that her
attention did not wander from her task.

Harriet repressed a small smile as her cousin
sighed gustily. Poor Sophy, she was not overfond
of stitchery, but Lady Phoebe was adamant that
the ability to set a neat stitch was of paramount
importance to any young lady with the slightest
pretension to breeding!

The Hall was an old house, stone built, with

mullioned windows and a number of small rooms, much deplored by its mistress. For her part, Lady Phoebe would much rather have had a fine Palladian mansion in the style of Mr. Robert Adam, with a wide portico and a handsome wrought-iron stairway, instead of half a dozen sets of narrow winding stairs linked by a hodgepodge of rooms and passages. However, Sir George could not be swayed. No high-falutin' London architect was going to pull his home to pieces! It had suited every member of his family from Elizabethan times onward, and he was not going to change it now! Besides, he told his wife, small rooms were easier to keep warm— a considerable inducement to leave the house as it was, what with the expense of sea coal brought all the way from Newcastle, and the cold winds that blew in off the Marsh!

If Lady Phoebe could not have her way over the matter of reconstruction, she had at least introduced what she was pleased to term the "refinements of civilized persons" into the Hall in the shape of a handsome Brussels carpet and a full set of dining chairs and a table, ordered direct from Mr. Sheraton of London, via his illustrated catalogue. And her renovations had not stopped there. Thick velvet curtains of a rich plum shade now swept over the small windows, an extremely welcome improvement when the east wind blew up the estuary. Two or three very elegant console tables littered the salon which she had made her own, and in the room that she was now pleased to refer to the withdrawing room (previously, and still to the younger members of the household, the winter parlor!) reposed a very fine pianoforte, on which Sophy, who was no lover of music, was obliged to practice every morning.

This instrument was only one of the luxuries of the Hall sighed over by a slightly envious Harriet. She, who had a natural ear for music and a particularly fine voice, was obliged to content herself with the battered, out-of-tune pianoforte at the vicarage and be grateful that the coming of the new one had prompted Lady Phoebe to offer it to her parents.

Lady Phoebe raised her head to acknowledge Harriet's curtsy, frowning a little over her niece's windblown ringlets. Lady Phoebe did not approve of young ladies indulging in such vulgar pursuits as "walking." However, the lecture she was about to deliver was forgotten as her eye alighted on her newest acquisition, a very fine Egyptian daybed in striped burgundy and white satin. This handsome piece of furniture boasted feet carved in the shape of phoenix claws (all the very latest rage), and Lady Phoebe was only awaiting the right moment to display this stunning article to the awed admiration of her cronies. No one, not even the Duchess of Westchester, could boast such a very elegant sofa, so completely the *dernier cri!*

However, not even the highly satisfactory contemplation of this source of potential pleasure—her guests' envious stares—could keep Lady Phoebe from commenting rather waspishly on her niece's appearance.

"Harriet," she reproved, "you should have worn your bonnet. You look like a milkmaid!"

"Oh, Mama, how can you say so!" Sophy

cried indignantly. 'Milkmaids are always plump, with rosy cheeks—Philip says one can tell instantly that Harriet has good breeding because she is so fragile and delicate!"

Looking less than pleased at this observation, Lady Phoebe sniffed caustically. "I conjecture that your brother is comparing young ladies with racing horses!" And yet, she admitted to herself, there *was* an air of breeding about Harriet, much as she would have liked to deny it.

The two cousins were completely dissimilar, Sophy all pink and white softness where Harriet was as slender and graceful as a sprite. Sophy's huge blue eyes peeped flirtatiously at any unwary gentleman who chanced to pass, while Harriet's brown ones held an aura of remoteness for those who did not know her. Less forthcoming than her bubbling blonde cousin, Harriet was inclined to think Sophy the prettier of the two. It was true that Sophy's blonde prettiness tended to catch the eye, but Harriet's less obvious charm had an attraction for the more discerning that would outlast Sophy's girlish comeliness.

Gerald Willoughby did not encourage his daughter to indulge in the vice of vanity, and Harriet would have been surprised to hear her papa comment privately to her mama that in five years' time Harriet would eclipse her cousin. Elizabeth Willoughby agreed, although it made her heart sore to see her daughter obliged to make do with her cousin's cast-off garments, no matter how sunnily given. Of course, she never mentioned this to her husband, who had given up so much to marry her. Only she knew of the quite unexceptionable marriage that had been arranged for him by his grandfather—a match which would have more than made up for the deficiencies in his own small income. For herself, she was completely satisfied. She had Gerald and his love, but it did seem unfair that Harriet should be the one to suffer from their marriage, bearing her aunt's slights and her cousins' pity. In a more perfect universe, a kind fate might have so arranged matters that a handsome, well-endowed young gentleman would come along and offer himself to their daughter, but Elizabeth was worldly enough to admit that there was scant chance of Harriet's meeting any such person, circumstanced as they were as the Squire's "poor relations."

None of this worried Harriet. She knew that her parents were poor, but it had never troubled her, until now. The salon door opened, and her color came and went entrancingly as a young man with brown curling hair and teasing blue eyes walked in.

Lady Phoebe put aside her tambour frame and turned to observe her son. Even the most impartial observer could not help but notice the differing degrees of affection in which Lady Phoebe held her son and daughter.

"Mama dotes on Philip," Sophy would often comment, and unfortunately she was quite right. Although she prided herself on being a sensible parent, Lady Phoebe could not repress a small surge of pride every time she saw Philip. He was all that a good son should be—even-tempered, handsome without being foppish, clever enough for her to be able to boast of his accomplishments to her peers, and yet not so clever as to be ridiculously "bookish."

While it was not perhaps true to say that Philip had never caused his mama a single moment's alarm, he had certainly never driven her to the exasperated fury she frequently experienced with his sisters.

A young man of considerable intelligence and charm, Philip could hardly have remained unaware of his mama's partiality, and yet his fondness for his sisters was such as must always draw an approving smile from even the most critical of detractors. He was never unwilling to pander to a young lady's pleas for sweetmeats and stories, not too adult to indulge Sophy's love of hearing of the fashionable London society he now frequented. In fact, all at the Hall were unanimous in declaring that, if anything, Philip did not come home often enough, but as he had explained to his parents, if he was to carve a political career for himself as he hoped to do, he must be at the hub of things, making himself known and keeping his finger on the pulse of life.

Lady Phoebe agreed. Those who were accounted to know about such things were already saying wisely that young Wyclyffe promised to have a good political career in front of him at some time in the future. And certainly Sir George could not quibble at the admirable fashion in which his son managed to eke out the modest allowance he was able to make him. *He* need have no fears of Philip's gambling away his inheritance by issuing post-obit bonds on Sir George's estate!

All in all, Sir George and Lady Phoebe had

every reason to be proud of their son, although Lady Phoebe was wont to declare rather acidly that she was sure she knew not what of Sir George had gone into Philip's making, for in her view her son was all Butley! In this she did Sir George a great disservice. He might be a country squire, bluff and hearty, and perhaps more concerned with estate matters than fashionable tittle-tattle, but for those with the eyes to see, it was plain that in later years Philip would come to be just such an indulgent and caring landlord as his father and that much of the sunny temperament he shared with Sophy was Sir George's especial gift to his offspring. Of the trio, only Lucy, the youngest, was truly her mama's child, and it was hardly surprising that she was not a particular favorite with the two older girls.

Philip kissed his mama fondly, teased his sister, and then when Harriet was sure that he meant not to acknowledge her presence beyond a small smile, he stepped toward her, so plainly intent on soundly bussing her in much the same fashion, as he had Sophy that Harriet was rendered almost speechless with excited anticipation.

Lady Phoebe stared coldly at her niece and said, her voice as arctic as the north wind, "Philip, my dear, you forget that Harriet is no longer a child!"

These ominous words had the effect of making Harriet blush afresh, so embarrassed that she could not bring herself to look at Philip. Was it possible that her aunt had guessed her secret? Harriet prayed that it might not be so.

Lady Pheobe's cold disapproval reminded

Harriet afresh of the gulf that yawned between Philip and herself.

Her mama and Philip's father might be sister and brother. Her papa might be descended from one of the best families in the country. But Papa still had no title and little money, and was merely a country Vicar. Never had Harriet been so tremblingly aware of the disparity in their situations. She stared at the floor wishing wretchedly that she had never outgrown her childish worship of Philip and that her emotions were still safely cocooned in the innocence of youth.

Philip was regarding her with quizzical amusement. There could be no doubt how *he* had interpreted his mama's acid comment, Harriet thought in embarrassment. Plainly he was as aware as Harriet herself just how Lady Phoebe would react to his proffering the same token of affection to Harriet that he had done to his sister! But then Harriet was not his sister, however much he might have treated her as one in the past.

Ignoring his mama's quelling frown, Philip patted Harriet's cheek. "Does Harriet consider herself too old to be kissed by a mere cousin?" Philip asked his mother innocently, winking at Harriet.

"It is not a matter of what *Harriet* considers, Philip, but of what is correct," Lady Phoebe reproved majestically. "As I am sure you are aware, Harriet is now a young lady!"

"Yes, I can see that she is, Mama," Philip agreed gravely, amusement lurking in his eyes as they met Harriet's bashful glance. "And a very pretty one. Very well, then, if I am not to be allowed the felicity of a brotherly peck, then it will have to be a cousinly kiss!"

Harriet told herself he was only doing it to tease his mama, but she could not quell a tiny thrill of joy when Philip's warm lips brushed her cheek.

"Poor Mama," he whispered wickedly in her ear, "I swear she is ready to have an apoplexy!"

Despite the intoxication of his lips so close to hers, Harriet gave him a reproachful look. It was all very well for him to tease his mama so, but *she* would be the one to reap the harvest of his actions, and the look in Lady Phoebe's eyes when Philip at last released her did not bode well for their future relations. Harriet sighed. It was wrong of her, she knew, but she would have braved a hundred Lady Phoebes rather than give up the memory of Philip's kiss.

It was Sophy who broke the spell. She had been awaiting Harriet's visit in a fever of anticipation, and she was not going to be balked of her purpose now. If she was not careful, Philip would start talking about London, and then she would never be able to drag Harriet away. He had entertained them the previous evening with an account of the routs and balls he had attended, repeating a few of the milder escapades such as would not draw a censure from his strict mother. He had even launched into an enthusiastic description of a "mill" he had attended on Hampstead Heath until his mama had reminded him that her drawing room was not the place to regale them with the sordid details of a bout of fisticuffs, however much *gentlemen* might enjoy that sort of conversation.

Something of Sophy's anxiety showed in her eyes and her quick-witted cousin immediately guessed the cause. It was no secret to Harriet that Sophy was deeply in love with a certain Captain Edward Danvers, at present in command of a troop of militia garrisoned in Folkstone. Sophy had been presented to the Captain at Folkstone's Assembly Rooms during the winter assemblies, an occurrence which had promptly led Lady Phoebe to wonder if such occasions were, after all, quite as select as one might have supposed. The Master of Ceremonies had assured her that tickets were only issued to the most deserving of persons, but Lady Phoebe had remained doubtful, especially when she saw the fashion in which her impressionable daughter was regarding Captain Danvers!

Edward Danvers certainly had a most agreeable personality, Harriet allowed largemindedly, but secretly she did not consider that he in any way rivalled Philip! To be sure, the Captain presented an exceedingly fine figure in his regimentals, and seemed possessed of a considerable amount of charm and a decided sense of humor, but mere hazel eyes and medium brown hair could not be supposed to rival Philip's more dashing coloring.

As the winter months progressed, Harriet was alarmed, although not particularly surprised, to see Sophy's regard for the Captain grow. And she had to admit that Edward Danvers returned this regard. Only days after their very first meeting, he presented himself at the Hall, ostensibly to warn Sir George that the smugglers' activities were on the increase—the militia had been despatched to the Marsh with orders to disband the smugglers and put an end to the flow of contraband across the English Channel. A thankless and never-ending task indeed, as Captain Danvers told Sir George.

Apart from a few stolen moments alone between dances at the Assembly Rooms, when Lady Phoebe's vigilant eyes were elsewhere, Sophy had had scant opportunity to converse with her beloved, and Harriet, used to her frivolous cousin's intense but usually shortlived attachments, was beginning to become convinced that this time Sophy was sincere in her declaration that she loved Edward.

Naturally Lady Phoebe could not be expected to look complaisantly upon such a match. As little as she wanted a penniless Vicar's daughter for her son did she want a pecunious officer for her daughter, no matter how charming or pleasant he might be.

Sophy might sigh over Captain Danvers as much as she wished, her irate parent assured her spouse in the privacy of their bedchamber, but wed him she never would. Not whilst her mama had any say in the matter. Needless to say, it was but a short step from this announcement to the comment that she supposed she must lay the blame for this contretemps at her sister-in-law's door, putting ridiculous notions of "love" in her daughter's head!

Happily for Sophy's peace of mind, she was, as yet, unaware that her mama had discovered her secret. Lady Phoebe might rip up at her long-suffering husband for allowing the young man the freedom of the house, but she was far too long-headed to mention her feelings to a young daughter whom she had no compunction whatsoever in denouncing as far too fond of her own way to do anything but take bit into mouth and gallop headlong into goodness knows what mischief if her mama were to demand that she had nothing more to do with the Captain. No, Lady Phoebe devised a far more subtle method of detaching her daughter from the gallant Captain.

Informed by his spouse that she intended removing herself and her daughters to London so that the two young ladies might acquire the benefits of a little town "polish," Sir George had first expostulated at the expense and then cautioned his wife that she would find no better husband for their eldest daughter in London than she would among the good, honest, country society of their friends. Lady Phoebe remained adamant. Sophy was to have a London season, and if Lucy was too young to participate in the proposed treat, well, at least she would be a companion for her sister, and doubtless she would form connections which would stand her in good stead when she was old enough to be married.

Sir George might grumble about the shocking expense to his pocket and the materialistic outlook of his wife, but Lady Phoebe was adamant. To London they would go!

"Mama, may I take Harriet up to my room to show her my new gown?" Torn between a desire to have her ebullient daughter beneath her watchful eye, and a growing awareness of a certain something she could only think of as "dangerous" in Philip's attitude toward his cousin, Lady Phoebe gave grudging agreement, cautioning her daughter not to spend all day in her room chattering with her cousin, when there was still so much to be accomplished before they left the Marsh.

"Remember, Monsieur Lafayette will be here at two o'clock for your dancing lesson, Sophy. You were late last week, and he had to wait twenty minutes for you," she grumbled. "Twenty minutes while your father was paying him to sit in the gallery doing nothing!"

"Yes, Mama, I shall not forget," Sophy murmured demurely, whispering in an aside to Harriet, under cover of her hand, "honestly, Mama is the limit! Dancing lessons!" Sophy pulled a face.

Philip looked at his mother. "Dancing lessons? We are indeed become grand!"

"Sophy must be able to comport herself properly when we are in London," Lady Phoebe said repressively. "You would surely not want to be disgraced by your sister's performance on the floor."

"Certainly not!" agreed Philip with mock gravity. "It would quite blight all my hopes of ever becoming a politician!"

Even Lady Phoebe was obliged to smile at this witticism, albeit a little coldly. "It is not a funning matter, Philip," she scolded. "Sophy can never hope to get vouchers for Almacks if she cannot waltz!"

Philip raised his eyebrows a little at the mention of that hallowed building where the cream of the *ton* gathered twice monthly during the season to dance and gossip, partaking of an inferior, watery wine and thin, uninteresting sandwiches, while the newest clutch of young ladies paraded before their critical eyes.

A "Marriage Mart" some wit had once called it, and so it had remained, but for all the disparagement it received, only let one unfortunate young lady not receive the coveted voucher and nothing could ever remove the blemish from her reputation! An entrance to Almacks meant an entrance to high society!

Harriet stifled a small stab of envy. It was small-minded to feel jealous of Sophy, she told herself. Her father had lectured her long and often on the follies of the fashionable world, but she could not help reflecting rather wistfully how delightful it must be to whirl about Almacks' sacred floor, wearing a pretty gown, in the arms of a handsome gentleman (who somehow or other resembled Philip) while the musicians played the new and very daring waltz.

She came to with a start. Philip was smiling sympathetically at her, and Harriet blushed furiously. She hoped he had not read her foolish thoughts. As though to give the lie to this hope Philip cajoled his mama, "Is Harriet, too, benefiting from our French gentleman?"

"Certainly not," declared Lady Phoebe in outraged accents. "He is only teaching Sophy the waltz, and I cannot conceive that Harriet will ever need to know the steps, not when she is never likely to venture further afield than Folkstone Assembly Rooms!"

The words, unconsciously cruel, drove the color from Harriet's face. She knew, of course, that there was scant chance of *her* ever dancing at Almacks, but to hear it said and so very definitely, in her aunt's cold voice made the small pang of jealousy she had felt earlier deepen into a definite ache. Oh, not jealousy of Sophy precisely, she was too fond of her cousin for that! But if only she might have gone, too! Perhaps Philip guessed her feelings, for he corrected his mama.

"The waltz is all the rage. By the end of the year, it will have penetrated even to Folkstone. Besides," he coaxed, "what harm would it do to let Harriet learn alongside Sophy? She has little enough fun to look forward to. Her papa would disapprove, I am sure, but . . ." Lady Phoebe's eyes gleamed. Philip was right, Gerald would disapprove, but that did not weigh with her. Besides, she had no wish to appear less than charitable in her son's eyes. With the air of conferring a great favor, Lady Phoebe inclined her head.

"Very well, then, Harriet shall accompany Sophy to the gallery this afternoon, and if Monsieur Lafayette considers that Sophy is improving sufficiently for him to have time to spare to teach Harriet a few basic steps, then he may."

Almost overwhelmed by this unlooked-for condescension, Harriet stammered her thanks, while Sophy tugged at her gown.

"I must see you alone," she hissed in her cousin's ear. "Come now, before Mama starts to give us another lecture!"

No sooner were they in Sophy's room, the door closed safely behind them, than Sophy launched into a muddled and hurried tale.

"Harriet, the most dreadful thing. Edward . . . Captain Danvers . . . has been wounded, and I only heard of it by the veriest chance. Bill, my maid's intended, you must know—he is the gardener —well, that is to say, he is the *under*-gardener, you know how Mama is." She pulled a face. "Since the Countess hired a gardener who had been with Capability Brown, nothing would do for Mama but that she hired one as well, although Papa says he will not have the beech copse torn down, no matter how much it would improve the view, nor a lake excavated, for he says there is enough water, what with the sea and the dykes—oh dear, where was I?" she asked her cousin breathlessly.

"Telling me about Edward's wound," Harriet replied patiently.

"Oh yes, well, Bill heard about it when he went into Folkstone to collect some new fruit trees Mama had ordered from Kensington. The most dreadful accident—apparently the smugglers *set upon* poor Edward when he was riding out with his men the other night. And oh, Harriet, Edward sustained a ball in the shoulder, and is confined to his quarters!" Tears streamed down Sophy's face.

"If only Mama was not so worldly, we could have announced our betrothal and then I should be allowed to go and see him in a proper fashion, but instead . . ." She wrung her hands, staring piteously at her cousin. "You must see how it is with us, and I swear I shall positively *die* if I have to go to London without so much as a word of reassurance from him!" She clutched Harriet's arm. "Please help me, Harriet!"

"How can I?" Harriet asked her.

"Quite easily," Sophy replied, displaying an unexpected streak of practicality. "It would be the easiest thing in the world for you to take old Betsy and the trap and ride into Folkstone. Why," she declared ingenuously, "no one would think it odd in the slightest for you to be visiting Edward, for all the world knows you are forever visiting your father's parishioners!"

"But Edward is not a member of Papa's parish," Harriet pointed out reasonably, "and, Sophy, you can never have expected me to ride alone into Folkstone. Mama would never permit it, for one thing,'" she declared positively.

"Need she know?" Sophy coaxed artlessly. "Oh, Harriet, you are my last hope, see, I have writ a note already . . ." She rummaged in her workbox and produced a folded letter. "Please do it for me, *I* would do it for you!"

She probably would, Harriet admitted despairingly, suddenly feeling much older than her cousin, for all that Sophy was the elder by four months. But then Sophy did not feel toward her mama as Harriet did to her parents. *She* had been brought up in an atmosphere of loving trust, and the thought of deliberately deceiving her parents was complete anathema to her. (Her meeting with the smuggler did not count, for then she had been bound by her promise not to reveal their encounter, and even Papa, with his stern morals, would not quibble at that!)

Sophy eyed her speculatively. "Please, Harriet! How would you feel if it was Philip?" she asked with low cunning, laughing a little as the bright color suffused Harriet's embarrassed face.

"Oh, that was naughty of me, wasn't it? But I had to make you see how I feel. You have only to ride into Folkstone, visit Edward, and then ride back again. I have his direction. As a Captain he is allowed to lodge where he wishes." She pulled a wry face. "I tried to persuade him to show me his lodgings the last time I saw him in Folkstone, but he refused!"

Harriet stared at her cousin in awed fascination. "You mean you actually contemplated visiting a gentleman's room, unchaperoned?"

"Pooh, Harriet, you are too prim and proper," Sophy said scornfully, ignoring her cousin's disapproving expression. "Just wait until you are placed in the same position . . ."

"I trust I never will be," Harriet began faintly, allowing herself to be sidetracked. The argument continued for some time, Harriet demurring, and Sophy insistently pressing her cousin to capitulate, unashamedly reminding her of all the small kindnesses she had done *her* in the past, until at last Harriet started to relent.

"There!" Sophy began triumphantly. "It is not as dreadful as you seem to think." She looked up as feet clattered up the stairs. "Oh drat, that's Lucy, she sounds like a baby elephant. We can't talk while she's here!" Sophy pulled another face. "You know what she is, forever blabbing to Mama. Quick, before she comes in, tell me you will do it! If you do not, I shall go into a decline," Sophy threatened, "and then Mama will be forced to bring me back from London!"

Prosaically, Harriet pointed out that Lady Phoebe, no fond parent, was more likely to

37

lock Sophy in her room on a diet of bread and water, until she came to her senses.

"Oh, Harriet, why must you be so practical?" Sophy wailed. "Lucy will be here any second. Tell me you will do it?"

Harriet looked into her cousin's pleading eyes and felt herself weakening. "All right . . ." she said hesitantly, "but Sophy, I do not think . . ." She got no further. The door burst open and Miss Lucy Wyclyffe with scant ceremony addressed them both crossly, "So there you are. Talking secrets, I suppose! Well, I bet I can guess what they were," she said smugly.

Harriet sighed. Try as she might, she could not like Lucy. She was so like her mama. Completely indifferent to her cool reception, Lucy bounced into the room and sat down on a chair.

At sixteen Sophy was not properly out yet, but Lady Phoebe was of the firm opinion that nothing protected a young lady from importuning gentlemen, both welcome and unwelcome, quite so admirably as an attendant nymph, preferably in the shape of a garrulous and inquisitive younger sister, with a penchant for carrying tales to her mama's receptive ears.

Sophy eyed her sister with disfavor, exhorting her to take herself off and leave them alone. Lucy ignored this sisterly plea, declaring smugly that she knew what they were about and that if they did not let her stay, she would tell her mama that Sophy had been crying, and just because she had learned that Captain Danvers had been wounded.

"Have you been eavesdropping?" Sophy demanded menacingly, advancing toward her.

"Certainly not," Lucy returned promptly. "I heard Bill telling your maid. Mama does not know yet, but she will do soon." Lucy sniffed contemptuously. For her part, Lucy declared scornfully, she could find nothing to admire in a gentleman who allowed his men to be surrounded and trussed up like chickens by a mere half-dozen country bumpkins.

An unbecoming tide of scarlet filled Sophy's cheeks, and concerned lest the impending altercation bring Lady Phoebe upstairs to discover what was afoot, Harriet drew Lucy's attention to the new gown Sophy had just been about to show her.

It was the very latest fashion, high-waisted, with blue satin ribbon and tiny puffed sleeves, embroidered with lover's knots, but Harriet's attempts at conciliation were doomed. Lucy eyed the gown, and then her sister, seeming to Harriet's over-stretched nerves to take an inhuman delight in pointing out that the *gown* was "all right" but that Sophy, with her plump curves, would look a positive fright in it! Sophy's indignant protests were lost as Harriet's expression implored her to say nothing. With every evidence of satisfaction, Lucy extracted an unpleasant-looking boiled sweet from her pinafore pocket, put it in her mouth, and sucked it with a good deal of unnecessary and noisy relish.

Sighing, Harriet reflected that it was no wonder that Sophy and Lucy did not get on, not when Phoebe's notion of sisterly affection was to encourage the younger to tittle-tattle on the elder to such an extent that poor Sophy was driven to retire to the linen closet upon occasions, purely to escape her younger sister's too sharp eyes.

Apparently accepting that any further chance for private converse was now lost to them, Sophy picked up a copy of *La Belle Assemblée*, drawing Harriet's attention to the modes depicted therein with a casual indifference that did nothing to deceive their interested audience.

"You need not think you will get rid of me that way," Lucy announced forthrightly when her sister picked up yet another magazine. "I am to stay here until Monsier arrives. Mama says so," she announced with relish.

It was not until the clatter of horses' hooves in the stable yard, announcing the arrival of the dancing master, drew Lucy to the window, that Sophy had an opportunity to slip Harriet the all-important note. Harriet took it a trifle reluctantly, tucking it into her bodice.

"Don't let me down, I am relying on you," Sophy whispered fiercely as Lucy turned round.

Hurrying down to the gallery, Sophy begged Harriet to peep through one of the windows and observe Monsieur Lafayette. "Do look, he is so very grand, isn't he? I'm sure Mama thought he was an émigré of some distinction when she first saw him." Sophy giggled. "She would dearly have loved to boast to the Duchess that she had engaged a titled Frenchman to teach her daughter!"

Harriet laughed, albeit a little reluctantly. She could never bring herself to accept her cousin's devastatingly frank criticisms of her Mama, no matter how warranted.

Since Harriet knew nothing more than the most basic dance steps she had been taught by her mother, she smoothed her gown with nervous fingers as she stepped into the gallery, hoping Monsieur would not find her too clumsy a pupil.

Monsieur had been delayed downstairs. As chance would have it, he entered the house at the precise moment when Philip was leaving it, and suddenly recalling the purpose for which the Frenchman had called, the young man smiled mischievously and said to his mama, with assumed nonchalance.

"Do you know, I think I shall slip up to the gallery myself. After all I have seen the waltz performed at Almacks. I shall probably be able to give the girls some hints."

Lady Phoebe frowned, but there was little she could say. Certainly she had no wish to put any foolishly gallant notions in Philip's head by suggesting that she did not want him to be too friendly toward a girl he had hitherto considered very much in the light of an extra sister. Lady Phoebe hoped she was not that much of a sapskull!

On the pretext of desiring Monsieur Lafayette to spare her a few moments, she dismissed Philip to the gallery and having ascertained that he was safely out of earshot, she proceeded to instruct the dancing master that under no circumstances was Philip to be allowed to partner his cousin, especially not in the waltz.

Fully alive to the nuances of this command, the Frenchman mounted the stairs in some considerable trepidation. In his view, nothing was more likely to fan a small flame into a raging furnace than parental disapproval, especially when the young man concerned was as spirited as Master Philip appeared to be.

Harriet watched Sophy traverse the room on her brother's arm, while her instructor kept time and corrected her faulty steps. Her own initial longing to float over the floor held fast in Philip's arms had given way to terror that instead of gliding gracefully she was more likely to utterly disgrace herself by standing on his toes or committing some dreadful misstep.

Lady Phoebe's acidly sweet comment—that Master Philip must not be allowed to encourage his cousin's vanity by waltzing with her—very much to the forefront of his mind, Monsieur Lafayette was relieved to see that the young gentleman made no attempt to partner Harriet, instead guiding his sister about the floor to the accompaniment of giggles and stern admonishments every time Sophy missed a step.

Lucy's governess had been roped in to play the pianoforte, and somehow or other—the harassed dancing master was never quite sure how it had come about—Sophy was relegated to the role of observer while Philip masterfully swept Harriet into his arms when Miss Biddle struck up another waltz.

Monsieur Lafayette was horrified. After all his assurances to Lady Phoebe! But there was nothing he could do about it, short of dragging the culprits off the floor, and Harriet's bemused expression touched a tender chord in his heart. Poor child, it would do no harm, and she looked in need of a few carefree moments. Monsieur Lafayette sighed. Oh, to be one and twenty with nothing more on one's mind than love! Only a Frenchman could truly understand *l'amour!*

Harriet didn't care. All she was aware of was the heady delight of being in Philip's arms as they circled the floor, Philip occasionally pausing to murmur instructions, telling Sophy to watch her cousin's feet. Harriet had no time to feel nervous. With Philip's lips inches from her ear, her ringlets tickling his chin, as she listened earnestly to his commands she gave herself up to the joy of actually waltzing, and before too long she was able to follow his lead with quite a tolerable degree of composure.

"Excellent," he praised her when they came to a breathless stop next to Sophy. "Let's try again."

Harriet demurred, but it was a very half-hearted negative. Aided and abetted by a giggling Sophy, they took the floor again.

Harriet's gentle laugh rang out time and time again. Miss Biddle played until her arms ached. Monsieur watched unhappily as they whirled about the floor, uneasily aware that matters had slipped from his control.

At length Philip relinquished her, murmuring teasingly that he was quite sure she must rival the most accomplished female ever to grace a dance floor. Even Sophy forgot her problems long enough to participate in the fun. However, none of them were under the slightest delusion as to Lady Phoebe's reaction should she chance to enter the gallery, and for this reason Harriet's enjoyment suffered a blight. In a matter of three short days she had aided a smuggler to evade the course of justice, promised to act as a messenger in a friendship of which she knew her aunt disapproved, and now indulged in that shocking and very fast dance, the waltz, clasped tight in Philip's arms, when she knew full well that Lady Phoebe would have protested most strongly at this state of affairs. All in all, she reflected soberly, she had sunk almost completely beneath redemption!

chapter three

The unquestioning manner in which her mama accepted Harriet's request to be permitted the use of Betsy and the trap did little to alleviate the culprit's growing sense of guilt. She had not told a direct lie, Harriet assured herself uneasily, but merely allowed Mama to believe that the sole purpose of her excursion to Folkstone was the purchase of new ribbons for the bonnet she had been given by Sophy.

As it was only Tuesday, with two full days to go before market day, Folkstone was quiet. Harriet put off the evil moment as long as she could by dawdling over her purchases. Would the cherry ribbons look better than the green? As it was, she was still not sure she had made the right choice when she left the linendraper's.

Climbing back in the trap, Harriet urged Betsy forward. Folkstone was an old town full of narrow cobbled streets with odd twists and turns, some of them dangerously steep as they dropped precipitately down to the wharfs. As such it was admirably suited to add to the confusion and harassment of the Preventative Officers when they pursued their fleeing quarry—a quarry that, with a lifetime's experience of the town, could more often than not lead their pursuers a merry dance before finally eluding them. Small wonder, then, that these upholders of law and order were regarded with contemptuous amusement by those they would bring to justice.

Maneuvering the trap through the narrow archway that led to the street where Captain Danvers lodged was a more difficult task than Harriet had envisaged, and she decided at length to tie Betsy up outside a corn chandler's and complete the remainder of her journey on foot.

As she stepped down from the trap amidst curious glances from passers-by Harriet was reminded that Folkstone was not her papa's parish where everyone knew the vicarage trap and its occupant. Struggling with hampering skirts, it was some time before Harriet realized that some members of her audience were quite openly hostile. There was something intimidating about the small knots of bystanders; women garbed in black with cold, shuttered faces, knarled hands clasped over heavy woollen shawls; curious emaciated children clinging to their mothers' skirts; and the occasional gaunt fisherman, weathered and old before his time.

Harriet had seen poverty before—as her father's daughter, there was barely a cottage in the district she had not entered—but this was something different. On her uncle's estate even the poorest laborer had a patch of land to call his own where he might grow vegetables to supplement his meager diet, and Sir George was not one to make a fuss about the odd rabbit finding its way into someone's cooking pot. Folkstone was different. Here people's faces wore an ingrained look of apathy and poverty that had come from not just one or two bad winters but a lifetime of going without. Harriet's tender heart ached for them, especially for the children.

On the spur of the moment she had packed a basket of delicacies for the invalid, silencing her conscience by reminding herself that her mama had been disposed to favor the Captain and would surely have been the first to render him what aid she could had she known of his plight, even if it was only a cold veal and ham pie from the vicarage kitchen, some homemade soup, and an assortment of unguents and remedies for his wound. Now as Harriet lifted the basket from the trap she wondered if she had been wise. Speculative, greedy eyes coveted its contents and Harriet's hands shook a little as she marched firmly in the direction of the Captain's lodgings.

Sophy had given Harriet some breathless, garbled tale that the Captain had quarrelled with his relatives and was thus obliged to exist purely upon his pay, and Harriet wondered if this was possibly why he had chosen to lodge in one of the poorer parts of the town where every third building was an alehouse and the street grew progressively shabbier and meaner.

Her sensation of disquiet was heightened when she came upon a group of surly fishermen lounging against the breakwater. Keeping her face averted, Harriet hurried past. The old gown she had donned especially for the journey looked startlingly out of place in these surroundings, rather like Lady Phoebe wearing court dress to have tea with a cottager, Harriet suggested to herself, giggling nervously. Thank goodness! She was past those men!

Unfortunately she had relaxed too soon. Three or four children scuffling in the dust tugged at her skirts begging. Fear quickened her footsteps, but the children refused to release her, grubby fingers poking into her basket as eyes far too old and knowing, in pinched young faces, stared assessingly at their victim.

Harriet refused to panic. Someone would . . . someone *must* perceive her plight! She had been foolish not to bring the trap a little farther down the street, but then she had not realized it was quite so far to the Captain's lodgings. Anger lent her determination. Ignoring the children's taunts, she made to push past them, when a new voice intruded on the uproar, dispersing her tormentors like leaves in an autumn gale.

Relieved, Harriet turned to thank her rescuer. He was leaning against a wall, still wearing the same shabby frieze coat which she could now see had once been a deep blue before too much rain and wind had faded it to dull gray. He doffed his greasy cap, grinning wickedly at her dismay.

"Well, if it b'ain't the Vicar's daughter. A long way from home, b'ain't you, missie?"

Seeing him in the daylight for the first time, Harriet was amazed at the almost arrogant cast of his features, until, blushingly, she recalled her uncle once saying that the smattering of handsome, harsh-featured persons amongst the more homely fisherfolk of the community owed their existence to the late Sir Peter, who apparently during his lifetime had been vigorous in his attentions to his female tenants, with the result that a good many of their offspring bore his finely etched features. The smuggler must surely be one of that number.

His skin had an olive tinge, Harriet saw, but there was no time to take in any more because he was regarding her with a mixture of amusement and contempt that made her feel at a distinct disadvantage. The smuggler was obviously as much on his own home ground here as he had been in the wood, Harriet thought weakly.

"Well, aren't you going to thank me?" he asked softly.

Like one bemused, Harriet stammered, "Oh, yes . . . indeed . . . thank you!"

His sardonic smile did little to restore her equilibrium.

"What brings you to Folkstone, then?" He eyed her basket considerably, "More good works?"

"Of a kind," Harriet hedged, having no desire to reveal to him the real purpose of her visit. "I am visiting a friend. He has been ill . . . suffering from an acute disorder . . ." she improvised wildly when the smuggler's eyes commanded her to go on.

"This friend . . . he wouldn't be a Captain Edward Danvers by any chance, would he?" mocked the smuggler.

Harriet gasped and almost dropped her basket. "H-h-how did you know that?"

Her companion grinned.

"Oh, that would be telling, missie. You b'ain't going to tell him about the other night, be you?" he asked softly.

"You must know I would not!" Harriet told him indignantly. "Not when I have given you my word!"

"And your token," the smuggler reminded her.

Her token! How dare he remind her of that stolen kiss! Crimson with mortification, Harriet stepped past him.

"B'ain't you going to reward me for rescuing you, then?"

Harriet could not believe her ears.

"Reward you?"

"That's right, missie. After all, those young varmints would have had your basket emptied like lightning if I hadn't happened along, and then what would poor Captain Danvers have done, deprived of the fine victuals you are taking him?"

His voice was openly sarcastic, making Harriet wince as she remembered the children's thin arms and legs.

"I could not have fed them all," she began helplessly, shaking her head. "Captain Danvers is wounded . . ."

"I know all about that," he cut in curtly. "Well, missie, do I get a reward, or don't I?"

"I have nothing with which to reward you," Harriet began, only to break off when he laughed.

"You don't learn, do you, missie? I'll be pleased to take the same as I took before."

"You! No!" Harriet said firmly. "*No!*"

"That's a fine way to treat your rescuer! I warn you I mean to have my reward, whether it's given willingly or nay!"

"If you are so hungry for kisses, why don't you seek out some of the village maids?" Harriet asked him witheringly. For some reason or other she had the disturbing sensation that the smuggler was actually laughing at her!

"Perhaps I prefer kisses that aren't so readily given," the smuggler retorted promptly, bending to cup Harriet's chin with his hand. Hampered by her basket, she could do nothing but try to avert her face and glare furiously into the smuggler's laughing eyes.

"Doubtless women of your own sort are attracted to your uncouth wooing, sir," she told him freezingly, "but it finds no favor in my eyes!"

"My, that's a fine speech," he marvelled wonderingly. "You're full of pluck for such a tiny little thing, but you shall not deny me my reward!"

And he was quite right, as Harriet very soon discovered. It was true that his lips were not quite as punishing as they had been upon that other occasion; indeed, they had a tendency to linger deliberately over the kiss as though he derived a wicked enjoyment from prolonging her humiliation, Harriet thought vexedly.

However, at last she was free, the smuggler betraying no more contrition than had he been indulging in some gallantry with a woman of his own class, and Harriet refused to give him the satisfaction of seeing how much the encounter had upset her.

The smuggler folded his arms and watched her sardonically. "The captain lodges over yonder, missie. Fear not, nothing shall harm you whilst I am here!"

The arrogance of the creature! Harriet seethed with longing to tell him that she feared naught, not even him, but somehow lacked the courage. She only hoped she never had the misfortune to meet him again!

Harriet was still flustered when she was shown into the Captain's room by his taciturn landlady. He was sitting up in bed, propped up with a pillow, his wounded arm swathed in bandages, looking interestingly pale. He looked up when the door opened, staring in astonishment at his visitor.

"Why, Miss Willoughby! This is an honor I had not looked for!" His surprise only added to Harriet's agitation.

"Oh, no, I am only come as a messenger! That is . . . I am come from Sophy," she said, at last taking a grip on her scattered wits. "She heard that you were wounded and nothing would do but that she send a message to you."

Her wry words made the Captain smile understandingly.

"I'll wager she gave you no peace until you agreed to be her emissary, if I know my Sophy."

Harriet did not disagree, and the Captain laughed.

"She is a wretch, Miss Willoughby, but I must admit that on this occasion I am delighted that she got her way." He frowned a little. "I hope you will not misunderstand when I say that I am glad Sophy herself did not venture into these parts."

"No indeed, sir," Harriet agreed heartily. "It would never do for the daughter of Sir George to . . ."

"No, no, you misunderstand," Captain Danvers broke in hurriedly. "I did not mean to imply any difference between your stations in life. I have experienced too much of that myself to inflict it upon anyone else," he added wryly. "No, what I meant was that while you as the daughter of a Vicar have at least some knowledge of how the poor must live, my present dwelling must surely come as the greatest shock to my lovely Sophy, who has not the slightest realization of my true straits, bless her. You will not credit it, Miss Willoughby, but the darling actually suggested that we could marry and live on my *pay*, and with only one of her pretty gowns costing more than I earn in a twelve-months!"

Harriet sympathized. She knew Sophy had not the slightest inkling of economy or how to run a household, but she had no desire to depress the poor Captain any further.

"Sophy has been a little spoiled," was all she would say, quickly changing the subject and handing the Captain Sophy's note. Perceiving that he was itching to read it, Harriet wandered over to the window, staring discreetly through it while the Captain broke the seal and perused his letter.

From her vantage point she could see the wharfs and the fishermen lounging against their boats as they waited for the tide to turn. Was the smuggler amongst them? Firmly Harriet quelled her curiosity. What did it matter to her *where* he was, so long as he did not again intrude upon her life?

Edward Danvers did not seem as down-hearted by the news of Sophy's imminent departure as Harriet had expected him to be, but an explanation was soon forthcoming. His Colonel, an excellent man, had suggested that he might recuperate more readily from his wound in the bosom of his family, where he might receive all the little attentions and luxuries so necessary to an invalid's rapid recovery.

Edward had been forced to admit that his sole living relatives comprised a cousin, who was presently serving with Wellington in the Peninsula, and a grandfather from whom he was at present estranged. The Colonel was shocked, and, as Edward did not scruple to tell Harriet, he had enquired straightway if his Captain would allow him to endeavor to mend matters with his grandfather.

"I collect he thought it was some youthful folly, gambling debts or some such thing," he told Harriet ruefully.

"But it isn't?" Harriet asked, curious in spite of herself.

Edward shook his head. "A common enough tale; my grandfather did not approve of my father's choice of wife. The last time we met, such things were said, such insults traded, and such aspersions cast upon the characters of my parents that I am morally obliged never to enter my grandfather's house ever again."

"Oh, but surely," Harriet protested, "angry words spoken in the heat of the moment, instantly regretted . . ."

Edward shook his head regretfully. "You do not know my grandfather!"

"But you *are* his grandson."

Edward pulled a face. "So the Colonel reminded me. He wrote to my grandfather, although he did not tell me of it until later, and the result is that I am to recuperate in his care."

"After you threatened never to darken his door again," Harriet said sympathetically. "Oh, poor Edward, but I am sure it is for the best." She looked doubtfully round the shabby little room. "I am sure you will receive better care than you are doing here."

"Oh yes, I shall have the whole household running round me," Edward agreed carelessly, "but *that* is not why I agreed to go."

"Oh?"

Edward smiled mischievously. "My grandfather, Marquis of Rochester, has determined to open his London house for the duration of the celebrations to mark the Regency, and it is there I am bound once my arm has healed enough for me to travel!"

"London!" Harriet's eyes widened. "But

that means you will not be parted from Sophy! Oh, Edward, she will be so relieved."

Edward flushed uncomfortably. "Miss Willoughby, you must be thinking me the greatest rogue alive," he mumbled. "To encourage Sophy to hope that there might be some future for us when all the time I *know* I shall never be in a position to offer for her, but she is so lovely, so adorably sweet, so . . ."

"But your grandfather—"

"No, he will do nothing," Edward told her simply. "The day my father married my mother he cut him out of his will, and I am not the eldest grandson, you know. My cousin, Roger, is his heir." He shrugged fatalistically. "I am not going to pretend it would not advance my case with Lady Phoebe were I to allow her to believe I had some expectations from my grandfather, but I will not deceive Sophy's parents, not even for that!"

Harriet found herself liking him more and more. He had a stern streak that she felt would be a good influence on Sophy, tempered as it was with a kind disposition and a sunny temper. But sympathetic though she was to the lovers' plight, Harriet could not see any happy outcome for them, any more than she could for her own burgeoning love for Philip.

It was while Harriet was so charitably engaged on her cousin's behalf that an alarming discovery was made at the Hall. Miss Biddle, wondering why her young charge had not presented herself for her afternoon walk, went upstairs to find Lucy lying on her bed, cheeks

56

hectically flushed while she scratched crossly at the small red bumps on her arms and legs.

"Chicken pox," pronounced Doctor Barnes, answering an urgent summons from an irate Lady Phoebe. "Keep her warm," he told that good lady cheerfully, "feed her on thin gruel, and keep the rest of the household away from her. Oh, and make sure she does not scratch. It will all be over within a month."

"A month?" Lady Phoebe repeated, outraged. "But we leave for London at the end of *this* week! All the arrangements have been made, the house hired and aired!"

She followed the doctor downstairs, vigorously denouncing Lucy's selfishness at disobliging her mama by contacting such a childish ailment at this particular time. Doctor Barnes was amused but did not show it.

"Well, one thing's certain. She cannot go to London," he told her, enjoying the spectacle of Lady Phoebe's affronted expression. "And you had best keep her away from her brother and sister," he added with malicious amusement, "otherwise they will take the ailment from her!"

Half an hour later, when Lady Phoebe had exhausted her household by voluable repetition of her indignation at the ill turn fate had served her, it was Sir George who suggested mildly that if she was so anxious to have a companion for Sophy, she could do far worse than take Harriet in Lucy's stead.

At first inclined to reject the suggestion out of hand, Lady Phoebe was only persuaded to see the sense of her spouse's idea when Sir George pointed out the advantages of bringing both girls out at once, remarking wisely that to do so could only reflect upon his lady to her credit.

"Depend upon it, my love, you will be praised to the skies for such a very generous action. It will cost you naught, after all!"

"Naught?" Lady Phoebe sniffed. "That's all you know of it, sirrah, with Harriet without so much as a respectable stitch to her back."

Sir George congratulated himself. He had long wanted to do something for his sister's child, and now he saw his chance.

"As to that," he said genially, "the estate has done well this year, and I dare say I can spare a few guineas for fripperies for Harriet. Besides," he added craftily, seeing the denial hovering on his wife's tongue, "there must be plenty of young Sophy's gowns which could be made over to fit her cousin. She has enough of them."

Lady Phoebe abhorred waste. Her eyes narrowed thoughtfully. Certainly it would be very useful to have Harriet there to keep Sophy out of mischief, and if Sir George's guineas could be stretched to include a new bonnet and gown for herself . . . Lady Phoebe inclined her head majestically. "Well, well, Sir George, but I want it made plain that Harriet accompanies us primarily as a companion for Sophy," she warned.

A note was penned and sent round to the vicarage. As Lady Phoebe told her husband, it was hardly to be expected that his sister would scorn such a chance for her daughter—a veritable chance in a lifetime! Due to the unfortunate circumstance of Harriet's being so nearly related to Sophy, there could be no question of her remaining discreetly in the background, forbidden the treats enjoyed by the other girl, as Lady Phoebe would have preferred, and who could tell what the result might be? A season in London, in such an exciting year as this, the first of the Regency, promised to be . . . Harriet might achieve a very creditable alliance indeed, with all the world and his wife going to London for the celebrations.

Indeed, Lady Phoebe reflected, it would be no bad thing if she took a hand in actively promoting a match for her niece. That way there could be no danger of Philip contracting any *mésalliance* with the girl.

The more Lady Phoebe pondered this point, the more convinced she became that Harriet's inclusion in the party was all for the best, to such an extent that before the dinner gong sounded, she was smugly congratulating herself on so speedily solving the problem caused by Lucy's unexpected illness.

Lady Phoebe's letter had already been the subject of quite heated discussion at the vicarage long before Harriet returned home. Elizabeth Willoughby hoped she was not a doting mama, but it had long been her belief that her pretty Harriet was worthy of better things than marriage to some dull farmer or country lawyer, which was the best she could hope for in their present circumstances.

Harriet's papa, on the other hand, while not wishing to forbid Harriet a treat, was concerned lest such a visit give his daughter worldly ideas, such as dominated her aunt's life, or made her dissatisfied with her own relatively humble station in life.

To this Elizabeth replied with unusual tartness that with Harriet's looks and charm, she might well find at the end of the season that she had a very different future to look forward to, asking her husband a little bitterly whether he could countenance his child marrying his curate, or one of the wealthier farmers' sons, for this was the fate that must surely be hers. Her husband was horrified. He himself placed no great importance on rank, but there was a vast difference between a *gentleman* and a country farmer. He needed little further persuading. Their daughter, Elizabeth reminded him, had the benefit of their teaching to fall back on and a sensible head on her shoulders, for all her lack of years. The Vicar sighed. "You do not think she is over-young?"

Elizabeth smiled. "She is exactly a year younger than I was when I saw you for the first time and knew I had fallen deeply in love for all time!"

Arriving home to the startling information that she was to leave for London at the end of the week, Harriet did not at once assimilate the full import of Lucy's illness.

A note of acceptance was penned to Lady Phoebe. The Vicar took his daughter into his study and delivered a stern lecture on the follies of placing too much importance on fashionable life. However, he did unbend sufficiently at the end of it to kiss Harriet on the cheek and remark benignly that he knew he could be proud of her. Harriet fled, close to tears. Behind the closed door of her bedroom she vowed that she would do everything in her power to live up to Papa's faith in her, even to the extent of forgoing the wearing of her new bonnet in church on Sunday, recognizing in her new wisdom that the object of that exercise had not been to venerate God, but to draw Philip's admiring eye.

Fortunately this mood of self-denial did not last very long, and the bonnet with its new cherry ribbons duly got its airing, although Harriet did not get much opportunity to observe its effect on Philip, as Sophy pounced on her cousin immediately she stepped outside the church to ask in a hissed undertone whether Harriet had managed to deliver her note.

Poor Sophy! Anxious to ensure that her elder daughter did not succumb to the younger's illness, Lady Phoebe had kept Sophy strictly within doors, even banishing Harriet from visiting lest the other girl had picked up the affliction on one of her visits to her father's parishioners. Fortunately this had not proved to be the case, and while Lucy was confined to the schoolroom, Lady Phoebe relaxed sufficiently to allow the two cousins to meet, remarking in an arch tone to Harriet that she was sure she must be looking forward to her unexpected treat. Miss Biddle, overhearing the latter comment, chirped up gushingly that Miss Willoughby was the luckiest girl, to have such a very generous relative, a comment which did her no good at all in Harriet's eyes and earned her a reproving frown from Lady Phoebe, who commented acidly that she was surprised that Miss Biddle had felt able to leave the invalid.

"Oh, dear . . . but it is Sunday, and I do hate to miss church. I am not infectious, for I have already had the chicken pox . . ." Her voice trailed away unhappily as Lady Phoebe continued to regard her with an unwavering stare.

"Thank goodness for that," Sophy whispered to Harriet. "Now Mama will bully her all the way back to the Hall and you can tell me all about Edward." She squeezed her cousin's arm. "I'm so pleased that you are to come with us instead of Lucy, Harriet, and so is Philip!" She saw her cousin blush and laughed delightedly. "There, I knew you had conceived a *tendre* for him."

"Hush, not so loud!" Harriet glanced anxiously over her shoulder. "Your mama will hear, and she will not approve."

"Oh pooh. Mama does not approve of anything. Don't let her upset you, Harriet! Quickly now, tell me, how is Edward?"

Obligingly Harriet repeated her conversation with Captain Danvers, happiness bubbling up inside her. She was actually going to London. She would see Philip every day—well, nearly every day, for although he had his own lodgings in Half Moon Street, he was bound to call on his mama. Harriet sighed blissfully.

chapter four

"Sophy, do sit still," exclaimed Lady Phoebe in exasperated accents. "I swear it is fatiguing enough travelling over these deplorable roads without you continually bouncing about!"

"The journey will soon be over, Mama," Philip comforted her. "I can see the dome of St. Paul's."

Naturally this observation had both Sophy and Harriet crowding excitedly against the window.

"Where, Philip? I can't see it," Sophy complained.

"Wait until we turn the next corner. You will have a better view then," Philip advised her patiently.

"Well, I, for one, am just thankful that our

journey is at an end," Lady Phoebe declared, although her relief was short-lived when Philip told her that it would take them the best part of an hour to negotiate the London traffic.

In the event, his prediction proved quite correct. Dusk was just beginning to veil the streets when they drove through Grosvenor Square. Harriet was amazed to see a number of elaborate iron contraptions flowering at regular intervals along the paved walkways.

"What on earth are those?" she asked Philip.

"The new gas lamps," he replied promptly. "They are all the rage, although some people complain that the fumes they give off are offensive, but they certainly give a far better light than the old flambeaux. Wait until you see them lit."

When they eventually drew up outside their destination in South Audley Street, Lady Phoebe was not in the best of moods. Never a good traveller, she swept her daughter and niece before her and glared disparagingly at the tall, narrow house facing them.

"And they call this a *gentleman's* residence!" she pronounced in tones of bitter sarcasm. "Why, it is no more than shabby-genteel at the best!"

"It is an excellent address, Mama," Philip insisted soothingly. "And I promise you, you will find it quite roomy. These houses have a narrow frontage but stretch a long way back!"

Lady Phoebe sniffed. An impressive footman opened the door and ushered them in. Lady Phoebe stared round the oblong hallway, while Harriet and Sophy exchanged mute looks. Unable to find any fault with the black and white tiled floor, nor the airy wrought-iron staircase, Lady Phoebe progressed to the first floor.

Here she allowed that the two withdrawing rooms could be thrown together to make a very tolerable ballroom, although she could never like the wallpaper in the dining room. Red had never been one of her favorite colors.

The third floor offered four adequate bed-rooms and a small but serviceable room which Lady Phoebe declared would do admirably for the sempstress she intended to hire to make the girls' gowns. Thrifty to the core, she had no intention of wasting her guineas on expensive modiste-bought creations when the very same thing might be had at a fraction of the cost by judicious studying of the fashion plates in the *Ladies Journal* and the services of a good needle-woman.

At last, having completed her inspection, Lady Phoebe allowed that the house would "do," although how on earth she was supposed to manage with a bedchamber without the space to swing a cat, she really could not say.

It was just as well that Philip had accompanied them. He knew just how to handle his mama. While Harriet summoned her maid and instructed her to prepare a tisane for her mis-tress, Philip assured his mama that she would find the house typical of those hired out for the season and coaxed her into a good humor by telling her she would find herself with so many invitations that he doubted she would ever see her room, never mind find the time to swing a cat in it—which he was sure was a very shocking thing to do, anyway, and not like his mama at all.

This raised a slight smile, and by the time the maid returned with the tisane, Lady Phoebe was ready to allow that nothing could have been more tasteful than the green and gold décor of the drawing room and that the small blue sitting room would do very well for the girls' use, when they were not entertaining.

After that it only needed the butler, a person of undoubted perception, to advise her that he had instructed cook to prepare a meal to tempt the palate of even the most discerning of people, to assure Lady Phoebe that, contrary to her initial impression, there was no need to post straight back to the comforts of the Hall and totally abandon the very notion of remaining in London.

"Thank goodness for that!" Sophy whispered to Harriet. "Just imagine, to return to the Marsh now, when Edward will soon be arriving!"

Privately Harriet echoed her sentiments, although for different reasons. Anywhere where Philip was would be heaven to her, but she could not quite quell a tiny quiver of excitement as she knelt by the window and looked out over the city. London, capital of the fashionable world . . . she would have been less than human not to feel any thrill at *that* thought!

The morning found Lady Phoebe restored to her normal spirits. Adjuring Sophy not to dawdle over her breakfast, she announced that she intended to devote the morning to shopping. Naturally enough, this entirely agreeable suggestion met with no opposition from the girls. By the greatest of good fortune Lady Phoebe had learned from Mrs. Fanshawe, who had but lately returned from London, that if one wanted a bargain, one could not do better than visit Grafton House.

Philip, who had stayed overnight to ensure his mama was comfortably settled in her new abode, looked a little doubtful. "It will be full of cits, Mama. I do not believe it is frequented by persons of quality."

"It is also a good deal cheaper than the fashionable modistes, Philip, and although your papa has been very generous, with gowns to buy for both your sister and Harriet" (a look in Harriet's direction reminded her niece of just how beholden to her relative's generosity she was), "I have engaged a sempstress, the butler's niece, apparently, and she will accompany us. Her name is Fitch. If you are quite finished toying with that bread and butter, Sophy, we shall go!"

Their first port of call was Hardings, on Pall Mall, but after little more than a cursory inspection, Lady Phoebe declared that the fabrics were quite inferior and hustled her charges in the direction of Layton Shears, where she had been assured it was sometimes possible to see members of the King's household purchasing fabrics for the Princesses.

Certainly the drapers carried an excellent range of fabrics. But they were only to look, mind, Lady Phoebe warned, and then they would repair to Grafton House to select their materials. Sophy pouted a little. She had hoped to have at least one gown from the fashionable

Celestine's, but her mama soon depressed these notions by remarking rather acidly that if Sophy knew where she was to get upwards of a hundred guineas for one dress, then she was welcome to do so!

As it was quite early, Layton's was practically empty, a veritable treasure cave of fabrics of every conceivable color and texture, bolt upon bolt of the stuff piled high upon the shelves. A very helpful gentleman brought chairs so that they might sit down, assisting them with a smile for the girls and a respectful attitude toward Lady Phoebe that immediately bolstered her opinion of him.

Sophy pointed to a deep blue gauze that had caught her eye, with intricate silver embroidery running down one side.

"A very pretty fabric and quite exclusive. It is French, and we have just the one bolt."

Harriet, who until that moment had been disposed to sigh wistfully over it herself, suddenly decided that it was quite the horridest stuff she had ever seen, and Lady Phoebe, with one eye on the price, declared firmly that she did not believe in buying smuggled goods. By the time the gentleman had recovered from this leveller, the ladies were on their feet and through the door.

The sempstress, conscious of her uncle's admonition that if she pleased Lady Phoebe she could soon be well on the way to setting up as a modiste in her own right, if she would be be advised by him, had taken the precaution of acquiring several copies of *La Belle Assemblée* and the *Ladies Journal* and now tentatively expressed the opinion that it was not a task outside her powers to contrive some very creditable copies of those fashions for her clients.

A judicious glance at the fabrics lining the draper's walls had reaffirmed this conviction. As Lady Phoebe led the way to the waiting barouche, Fitch was able to comment very knowledgeably indeed about the possibility of amber crape making a very pretty walking dress for Miss Harriet, with perhaps a demi-toilette of mulled muslin for both girls, and of course, the pale blue velvet—a *must* for Miss Sophy—a pelisse perhaps trimmed with swansdown, with a matching bonnet, and for Miss Harriet, the rose velvet, an admirable foil for one of her dark coloring.

Before they could reach Grafton House, however, Sophy, leaning from the barouche in a fashion which her mama denounced as quite vulgar, spotted the Pantheon Bazaar and nothing would do but that they stop the carriage so that the girls might explore this delightful mart. Lady Phoebe, inclined to refuse, changed her mind when Fitch exclaimed knowledgeably (thank to the *Ladies Journal*) that this excellent emporium sold silk stockings for *less* than twelve shillings the pair!

An hour later, having indulged to the hilt the eternal female passion for bargains, the four ladies emerged from the Mart the richer by several pairs of stockings, at the truly ridiculous price of eleven shillings the pair, several elegant ostrich feathers to trim a cap for Lady Phoebe, and a very handsome Norwich silk scarf trimmed with silver spangles.

It was Harriet, catching sight of a monkey on a stick that walked when one pulled the string, who dashed back, insisting that it would be just the thing to send back to poor Lucy. Lady Phoebe, quite softened by this display of cousinly thoughtfulness, agreed to wait until Harriet had completed her purchase, and it was while she was waiting to be served that Harriet spotted the elegant lady in the pink carriage dress.

It was the dress that first caught Harriet's eye. Quite the very plainest gown and yet so striking; with a matching pelisse worn open over it, and a neat little round cape trimmed all round with dark, glossy fur. Harriet was quite entranced and resolved there and then that if Fitch could copy it, then before too long she might own just such an ensemble herself! (An ensemble that had she but known it came from the most exclusive modiste in all London.)

It was only when Harriet turned to hurry back to the carriage that she noticed the lady had dropped her muff (the same silkily rich fur that trimmed her cape). Scooping it up before it could become soiled Harriet hurried after her. She was nearly too late. The lady was on the point of entering her carriage, when a rather breathless and slightly shy Harriet caught up with her.

Conscious of her rather shabby appearance, Harriet was reluctant to accost the lady, but the recollection that had the muff been hers, she would have been sorely distressed to lose it, lent her the courage to say hesitantly, "Pray excuse me, but your muff. You dropped it. It is so very pretty, I was sure you would not want to lose it!"

The lady turned, apparently undismayed at being addressed by a stranger, her eyes widening when she beheld her muff.

"Oh no! How careless of me." She stepped down from the carriage. "Surely you are not alone!"

Harriet shook her head, suddenly tongue-tied in the presence of such an obviously elegant personage. She was just about to reply, when Lady Phoebe, on the point of chiding Harriet for keeping them all waiting on the flagway in a keen wind, bustled up, pausing when she saw that her niece was engaged in conversation.

The lady looked up and saw her. "Your daughter has been so kind as to rescue my muff. I was just thanking her. Another girl would not have been so thoughtful!"

By the time that Lady Phoebe had explained that Harriet—a good child—was her niece and that Sophy was her daughter, the ladies were well on the way to becoming fast friends. It only needed Lady Phoebe to mention Harriet's papa, and their new acquaintance was recollecting having met him at her own come-out longer ago than she cared to remember!

"But I have not introduced myself," she apologized, going on to remedy this oversight. "I am Lady Burbridge. My husband is attached to the Foreign Office and we are come to London for the celebrations."

Alas no, she replied to Lady Phoebe's questioning. She had no daughters, nor even nieces. She eyed Lady Phoebe consideringly. She had no wish to cause offense, of course, but it oc-

71

curred to her that her new friend might not know many people in London.

A shade hesitantly she offered the information that she was a close intimate of Lady Sefton, one of the patronesses of Almacks, as Lady Phoebe must know. Naturally, she had no desire to be thought pushing or encroaching, but she would dearly love to repay Harriet's kindness and she could think of no better way than by bespeaking from her friend the much coveted vouchers for the subscription balls.

Lady Phoebe expressed herself overwhelmed by such consideration. Already her busy mind was working rapidly. Such a connection would stand them all in good stead. With the Burbridges, so obviously well connected in Government circles, all sorts of doors might open for Philip, and not just Philip. With Lady Burbridge's patronage, the girls' successful debut was more or less assured! She smiled her gratitude. Lady Burbridge was too kind. Both girls would be thrilled to receive vouchers for Almacks.

As though to confirm this statement, both Harriet and Sophy broke out into incoherent protestations of delight.

"Very pretty," Lady Burbridge said indulgently. "You are to be congratulated, Lady Phoebe, on two such very charming charges. We are to hold a rout party—a very small affair, you must understand, merely to welcome certain members of the Bourbon King's train to London. You will know that Prinny has begged the exiled French King to honor London with a visit, of

72

course. As a member of the Foreign Office it is Lord Burbridge's duty to entertain some of the Bourbon party. I fear it will be a dull affair, but if you would care to come? I shall contrive to invite some young gentlemen, and of course you must bring your own son—Philip, didn't you say? Very well, then," she concluded in satisfied accents, when Lady Phoebe voiced her thanks, "I shall send cards, or better still, perhaps you would care to take tea with me? The rout party is over a week away. I shall be seeing Lady Sefton before then, so if you would like to call on me, I shall be able to tell you what progress I have made with the vouchers."

Naturally Lady Phoebe could find nothing to cavil at in this suggestion. Smiling, she gave her assent, hustling her charges back to the barouche. As they drove in the direction of Grafton House, she waxed most enthusiastic, almost eloquent in her praise of Harriet, much to that lady's surprise—quite forgetting that there had ever been a time when she had not wanted her niece to accompany them.

Indeed, her praise was so lavish that honesty forced Harriet to point out that the lady could just as well have turned out to be no one of any particular importance, but Lady Phoebe brushed aside this modest rejoinder. Harriet was the cleverest of girls, she declared firmly; at one stroke she had accomplished something which might otherwise have taken days of careful planning, for although Lady Phoebe had several acquaintances in town, they were not such as would mingle with the very highest in the land, to which set Lord and Lady Burbridge quite plainly belonged—witness only Lady Burbridge's conversation!

So pleased was she with her niece that she resolved there and then to sacrifice one of her own new gowns so that Harriet would be dressed as finely as their new circle demanded.

As it was, all three ladies found themselves so much in charity with one another when they eventually stepped into Grafton House that not even the bustling crowds and queues at the counters served to depress their spirits.

Sophy came away well pleased with her purchase of blue velvet—the quality was almost as fine as that they had seen in Layton's and only half the price—and they had been able to buy most reasonably a sufficient quantity of swansdown to trim it, plus a very handsome selection of muslins at three and sixpence the yard for morning dresses.

Additionally Lady Phoebe had graciously consented to the purchase of some pale blue crape for a walking dress for her daughter, and sea-green for one for Harriet, with matching merino pelisses for both girls and fur trimmings for the capes. Spangled spider gauzes in rose and cerulean blue were added for evening wear, with tiny pearl buttons, blonde lace, and quantities of berlin silk in blues and pinks for Sophy and the deeper rose and a soft peach for Harriet.

The morning was completed with a visit to the showrooms of Wedgwood and Byerley where Lady Phoebe purchased a very handsome dinner service of a small lozenge pattern in purple between lines of narrow gold, adding, as an afterthought, a couple of pale blue Chinese vases which would set off to a nicety the white plaster niches she intended to have set into the drawing room walls, once she returned to the Hall.

Philip, who had apparently spent the morning renewing old acquaintances and exchanging gossip at Brook's, arrived just in time to join the ladies for luncheon, when Lady Phoebe was able to regale him with a round tale of their doings of the morning.

"Burbridge, you say?" he mused. "I have heard of him, of course. They move in the very highest circles, you must know, Mama!" He leaned across the table to tease Harriet. "Who knows, cousin, you could find yourself rubbing shoulders with Prinny himself!"

"Oh, no! I should die of fright!"

Philip laughed. "No such thing! However, you need not fear—they are saying in the clubs that Burbridge is in Prinny's bad books at the moment. Apparently he was one of those who opposed the Bourbon's visit. It seems he is concerned that French agents will attach themselves to the Bourbon faction, trying to discover information that will aid Napoleon's armies should they ever invade us!"

It was a chilling thought, and for a moment the atmosphere round the dining table was very sober. Harriet was just about to remark that she had read in the *Post* that tighter security measures were now being enforced, when Sophy tossed her head and declared pertly, "As to that, Captain Danvers says that Boney is already invading us! Every time a boatload of contraband is landed on the South Coast, more English gold is pouring into his coffers!"

Lady Phoebe pursed her lips, informing Sophy that the opinions of a mere Captain Danvers were of no interest to her. Furthermore, she opined, fixing Sophy with a hard stare, now that they were in London, she must not forever be boring the company by rattling on about dull country matters, and even duller country acquaintances.

Sophy objected crossly that the Captain was the grandson of a Marquis. Indeed he was, her mama agreed, pointing out with a touch of asperity that Harriet's papa had been just as closely related to an Earl, and look what had happened to him! Biting her lip, Harriet stared through the window. It was humiliating to have the gulf between herself and her cousins reinforced in such a fashion. Philip darted her a sympathetic look that warmed her heart a little, although Sophy had lapsed into a sulky silence, cheering up only when she recollected that soon her beloved would be in London. That was something that would not please her aunt when she learned of it, Harriet thought wryly. Harriet could not help feeling a little depressed. To be sure, they had had a very exciting morning, and here was Philip disposed to make himself pleasant to his cousin and his sister, but there was very little lover-like about his regard, and Harriet was forced to the unwelcome conclusion that while Philip might flatter and tease her, he still regarded her very much in the light of a younger sister. Not a very happy thought for a young lady who yearned to be the object of a much less fraternal affection!

The days sped by. To Harriet it seemed she had barely had time to turn around, and already they had been in London four days! Of course, with every afternoon spent in the sewing room with Fitch, alternately being measured and trying on gowns, it was no wonder that she hardly had time to catch her breath. She had a nostalgic longing for the clean sweet air of the Marsh and the wind in her hair.

Philip unknowingly supplied an antidote to this mood of introspection when he called one morning to take the girls up in his curricle and drive them around the Park. Lady Phoebe was dubious. Their new gowns were not finished yet, and she had no wish for them to be seen abroad looking like a pair of country dowds. Philip reassured her. It was too early in the day for the Park to be full. The fashionable hour of five to six was the time for that. Unwillingly Lady Phoebe allowed herself to be persuaded, but only on the strict understanding that Philip bring the girls straight back to South Audley Street.

Philip's hand on her arm as he handed Harriet up into his phaeton gave her a small thrill of pleasure. She turned to thank him, disturbed to see him so obviously preoccupied with other thoughts. A little uneasily she sat down next to Sophy. It was unlike Philip to be so unforthcoming, but this morning his face wore an expression of constraint, and his manner of replying to their questions was terse, sometimes almost abrupt.

The Park was not completely empty. They passed a couple of nurses keeping an eye on their young charges as they bowled hoops over the grass, and in the distance they could see the old horse and rider. The morning had a sharp, clean taste, and the flower beds were full of spring flowers. Harriet's spirits rose.

They were some yards off the Stanhope Gate when Philip was hailed by a chubby individual with a cheery expression, seated astride a smart bay.

"Not going to introduce me, Wyclyffe?" he asked, with an admiring glance at the occupants of the carriage.

Laughingly Philip complied, warning the girls not to be taken in by the Honorable Toby's breezy manner.

"He is an outrageous flirt," he pronounced darkly, much to the young gentleman's discomfiture, as he blushingly disclaimed to be any such thing. Intimating to his friend in a mock threatening manner that had he not been accompanied by his sister and cousin, the Hon Toby would have known just how to refute such a very libellous statement, he edged his horse a little nearer to Philip's curricle.

"Is it too much to hope that I might have the honor of standing up with you both at one of Almacks' Monday evening subscription balls?" he asked bashfully.

Since that very morning had brought the requisite vouchers and a very cordial note in Lady Sefton's own hand, Sophy was able to explain blithely that they were but recently come to town and not yet in the social swim, affording

Toby the information that they were to attend Lady Burbridge's rout party in the not too distant future.

Watching her cousin's self-confident approach to their new acquaintance, Harriet longed to have a little more self-assurance herself. It was all very well for Papa to say that young ladies of breeding did not put themselves forward, but there was no denying that Toby was responding most enthusiastically to Sophy's giddy chatter. Harriet wondered wistfully if Philip would ever look at her with just such a bemused expression and then told herself reluctantly that she was obviously not the sort to engender such admiration in the male breast.

While Toby engaged Sophy in conversation, Harriet was free to luxuriate in Philip's sole attention, although to be sure he did seem to spend an unwarranted amount of time glancing over his shoulder. Watching him do so for the fourth time, Harriet observed another carriage approaching them from the opposite direction. A sporting curricle with glittering yellow wheels and a dangerously high-sprung body, it swept down on them, the four magnificent grays drawing it reminding Harriet of animals from a book of fairy tales rather than real live horses.

The curricle drew level with them. A lady and gentleman were seated in it, the gentleman's face obscured by the capes of his driving coat and the beaver hat he wore upon his head, but Harriet did catch a glimpse of his companion, a woman with hair the color of living flames, dressed in a carriage gown of dark green velvet, so dashing as to almost take Harriet's breath away. She stared, plucking at Philip's sleeve, "Goodness, Philip, who was that?"

His face was as white as parchment, and for a moment Harriet thought he must be ill. Toby, observing the occupants of the curricle, looked at his friend in disquiet.

"Steer clear of that one, Philip. In the words of Caro Lamb, she is bad, mad, and dangerous to know."

"For the girls' benefit he explained a little uncomfortably, "Lady Mary Carrington. She has rather a bad reputation where young men of Philip's genre are concerned."

"That is enough, Toby," Philip said tersely. "You will please not speak of Lady Mary in such a fashion in my presence!" The Honorable Toby looked concerned.

"No, forgive me, I should not have mentioned her at all in present company," he said, and it seemed to Harriet that was the faintest emphasis on the words "present company" that conveyed some hidden meaning to Philip, for he flushed a little and his mouth grew quite hard.

There was no doubt about it, Harriet thought wistfully, Lady Mary was very beautiful with her white skin and red hair, although somehow she could not think that Lady Phoebe would approve of her. She was still trying to puzzle out why she should be so convinced of this when Toby took his leave of them. He made his adieux to the ladies and then hesitated for a moment, plainly uncomfortable, while Philip watched him with an expression that both puzzled and frightened Harriet.

"You will remember what I said—about

Lady Mary, won't you?" he proffered a little breathlessly at last, and would have gone on to say more if Philip had not shot him a warning glance as he gathered up his horses' reins and set the phaeton in motion.

"I am not some green boy still in leading strings, Toby," he replied—a trifle curtly, Harriet thought. "I assure you I am well able to conduct my own affairs!"

"Aye, and some affair that will be!" Harriet thought she heard Toby mumble under his breath as he rode off, but she could not be sure.

How had her cousin met Lady Mary, and why did Toby so obviously disapprove of her, Harriet wondered as they rode back to South Audley Street.

Philip could have given her the answer to both questions. He had met Lady Mary at Drury Lane. They had emerged at the same time, and he had trodden on her gown. Naturally enough in the exchange of apologies that followed he had made himself known to her and she to him. She had laughed up at him, her green eyes glinting wickedly, so very different from the shy young girls he was used to, so very free and bold in everything she did and yet still retaining a hint of hidden depths, withheld, but waiting for the man who dared to plumb them.

As for Toby's disapproval! Philip checked a little and frowned, and Harriet, discreetly observing him, wondered why.

Married at sixteen and widowed at eighteen, Lady Mary had left a trail of broken hearts and gained an infamous reputation on her passage through society. True, the blame for that disastrous early marriage could be laid on her father's hands. He had been anxious to get her off his hands and had not realized that the gentleman he had chosen was far from being the wealthy person he thought him. When her husband died, the young widow found herself with no means of support apart from her wits and her beauty, and these she used to excellent advantage. It was even rumored that at one time she had been Prinny's mistress, and that of the notorious Charles James Fox, Prinny's one-time drinking and gambling companion.

Certainly she was a woman with extravagant tastes, and a penchant for gentlemen who could fulfill them, although apparently she was not averse to encouraging the attentions of any gentleman who caught her eye, and many a young man had found himself caught in her toils, unable to break free of the spell of her beauty.

Philip knew all this, but it made no difference. The moment he saw her he knew, and he admitted to himself that he would move heaven and earth with his bare hands if it meant that he could bask in the glory of her smiles. He was behaving like a green boy, in love for the first time, he told himself wryly, but it made no difference. Whatever Lady Mary might have been, he was positive that she was the victim and not the aggressor. Like so many men before him, Philip was convinced that he alone knew her true character. Harriet, Sophy, his mama, all these were forgotten; Lady Mary filled his thoughts to the exclusion of everything else.

chapter five

"Harriet, when do you think I shall hear from Edward?" Since this was the sixth time Sophy had asked her that question in nearly as many hours, Harriet could have been allowed to feel exasperated by her cousin. However, she was far too kind-hearted to remind the other girl that since she was not possessed of special powers she had no way of knowing just why Captain Danvers had not been in touch.

"Perhaps his wound prevents him from writing. You may be sure he will be in touch the moment he is able, Sophy."

Somewhat mollified, Sophy admitted that perhaps she was being a little over-anxious.

"Mama is all of a twitter over this rout party

tonight, isn't she? Do you suppose the Burbridges will be very grand?"

"Philip seems to think so."

"Pooh, Philip!" Sophy shrugged with sisterly scorn. "I don't know what's amiss with him these days. Don't you think he's changed, Harriet?"

"He does seem a little preoccupied," Harriet allowed in a stifled little voice.

Poor Harriet. Far from bringing her closer to Philip, her stay in London seemed to be widening the rift between them—a rift which had suddenly sprung up following their ride in the Park, when Harriet had innocently and unwisely commented that Lady Mary seemed to be very popular with the gentlemen.

Lady Phoebe, on her way to her bedchamber to dress for the rout party, put her head round Harriet's door and seeing the two girls chattering, chastised them roundly, reminding them that they were promised at Lady Burbridge's for ten o'clock and it was already gone seven. She stared at little reprovingly at her niece.

On Lady Burbridge's recommendation, Monsieur Rochas had been requested to call at South Audley Street, and the result was that both girls now sported the new, shorter hairstyles. On Sophy the style was undeniably pretty, but the real surprise was Harriet. The artlessly tumbling ringlets, secured on the top of her head, revealed a delicate, slender neck, giving her features a fragile, almost fey appeal, her pansy-brown eyes almost too large for the dainty purity of her oval face. Her niece, Lady Phoebe realized with astonishment, was a beauty!

Tonight the maid had threaded silver ribbons through Harriet's curls to match the embroidered acorns on her dress of peach gauze. Never had Harriet possessed such a dress, nor dreamed she might.

She had seen the sketch in the *Ladies Journal,* a simple enough design, starkly Greek with a slender fall of skirt and tiny puffed sleeves. Whether Fitch had observed her look she did not know, but almost as though by magic she had drawn Lady Phoebe's attention to the sketch, remarking that such a very plain design would be admirable for Miss Harriet, and a perfect foil for the more ornate gowns favored by Miss Sophy. Perhaps the word "plain" had done it—Harriet could not really tell—but certainly it was a misnomer when applied to the perfection of the peach dress. Next to it, Sophy's fussy blue spider gauze with its blonde trimming and bunches of flowers looked over-elaborate. Harriet fingered the material, smiling a little.

"You look a real treat, Miss," the maid whispered shyly, "and that color, it does become you!"

With this sweet praise ringing in her ears, Harriet felt she had no need to blush for herself when she took her cousin's arm and they walked downstairs together. A girl singularly lacking in vanity, Harriet would have been surprised had she known that most people would consider that of the two *she* was the more attractive. Certainly Lady Phoebe looked a little startled when they stepped into the hall. She had no wish for her niece to be turned out like a servant, but somehow from Fitch's description of the peach gown she had expected something a little less . . . well . . . elegant!

Lord and Lady Burbridge had a house in Cavendish Square, and although the new gas lights had long since lost their initial strangeness, Harriet was able to marvel at the quality of the light they diffused as a liveried footman handed them down from the carriage.

Although it was barely ten o'clock, the square was thronged with carriages, and as they stepped into the large hallway, Harriet stared around in awe. She had never seen such a magnificent house before. By comparison, the Hall was a mere country cottage!

A portrait of Lady Burbridge adorned one wall, the work, Harriet learned later, of Sir Joshua Reynolds, who had painted her in the first years of her marriage. Various other portraits lined the walls, but since Harriet could not recognize any of their subjects, she did not find these particularly interesting. A good many persons seemed to be milling about in the hall, soft-footed servants very much in evidence as they removed capes and pelisses and ushered the guests into a large withdrawing room.

Harriet felt as though she had stepped into the pages of a fairy tale. Light from what she thought must be a thousand chandeliers glittered on the assembled personages.

"Lady Phoebe, please, come and meet my husband!" Lady Burbridge motioned to the tall gentleman standing behind her.

Lord Burbridge was a spare, graying man,

in his early fifties, good humor twinkling in his eyes as he smiled at Harriet. She liked him on sight, guessing that he was both an indulgent and a generous husband. Lord Burbridge, for his part, pronounced himself delighted to meet the young lady who had rescued his wife's muff, thanking Harriet gravely for preventing further depredations upon his purse! The twinkle accompanying these words wholly belied their meaning, and Harriet found herself laughing up at him without a trace of the shyness she had expected to experience.

Lady Burbridge's notion of a small supper party appeared to encompass the entire *ton,* and at least half of the diplomatic circle, or so Harriet thought as she stared about her in bemused wonder.

An excellent supper had been laid out in one of the rooms leading off the ballroom, although Harriet was far too enthralled in watching the lively scene around her to think about food. There were card tables, as well, Sophy informed her, so that the gentlemen would not be deprived of their favorite occupation!

They were introduced to so many people that Harriet's head was ringing with names.

"I shall never be able to remember half of them!" she confided to Sophy. "And I shall be terrified of getting them wrong. Just imagine addressing Lady Sefton as Lady Drummond-Burrell!"

"Or worse still, as Lady Jersey," agreed Sophy, mentioning another of the patronesses of Almacks. The thought of committing such a solecism had both girls dissolving into nervous giggles until Harriet recollected where they were and implored her cousin not to make her laugh.

They had been given orgeat to drink, much to Harriet's relief, for Papa rarely served wine at home—his stipend would not allow it—and on the rare occasions when she had been allowed this treat, Harriet had found it disappointing—such sour, dry stuff! She was not to know that Lady Burbridge, correctly estimating her young guests' lack of sophistication, had expressly ordered that the orange drink be made up and served to the younger guests.

Having bustled off to greet some new arrivals, Lady Burbridge returned, full of apologies for her laxness. "I have not yet introduced you to our 'lion' of the evening, have I? We are fortunate in having with us tonight a member of King Louis' entourage, the Comte de la Valle!"

Looking suitably impressed, Harriet stared obediently around the room until Lord Burbridge took pity upon her and commented in his dry fashion that the gentleman was probably making the most of his hostess's laxness by retiring to the card rooms. Judging by the tone of Lord Burbridge's voice, Harriet guessed that the Comte was not a gentleman it would be easy to overlook. Lady Burbridge's next words confirmed this impression.

"I am sure you will like him," she confided to Lady Phoebe. "The most charming of persons. A Frenchman to his fingertips, of course," she added, quite as though, Harriet thought indignantly, this set him apart from lesser mortals!

Lady Phoebe, who numbered two or three

impoverished aristocratic émigrés amongst her acquaintances, nodded her head. "Such a shame! His pockets are to let, I expect—that dreadful Corsican!"

Lady Burbridge looked surprised. "Impoverished, you mean? No such thing, I assure you. Of course, he has lost what lands the family held in France, and those were vast—the family rose to prominence in Francis I's time, you know," she added mysteriously, for all the world as though *she* was not expected to know what *that* meant, Harriet thought wryly. She had been well versed in history by her papa and knew quite well that Francis's method of rewarding his discarded mistresses with titles and lands had resulted in the founding of a good many of the French noble families.

"Fortunately," Lady Burbridge was continuing, "the family owned vast lands in the Indies and the American colonies. The Comte is a very wealthy man."

Harriet refused to be impressed. It was ridiculous to feel dislike for a man she had never even met, but she knew instinctively that she would not like the Comte.

She stopped to watch the dancers and lost the gist of Lady Burbridge's discourse until she heard her exclaim, "Oh, but I had quite forgot! Poor Edward. You must allow me to introduce your charges to him, Lady Phoebe. Quite the saddest tale!"

Through a gap in the crowds, Harriet observed the startling sight of her aunt being propelled toward a striped sofa upon which reposed the person of Captain Danvers, looking suitably invalidish, with a light rug over his knees and a gaggle of giggling girls clustered about.

She was just in time to hear Lady Burbridge declare gaily, "Edward was wounded by those wretched smugglers and has been sent home to recuperate!"

"Home?" enquired Lady Phoebe in fading accents, with a direful glare at her daughter, as though she believed her personally responsible for the Captain's appearance.

"Why, yes. My godfather, the Marquis of Rochester, is giving Edward house room—after all, he is his grandfather—but the poor boy grows lonely shut up in that huge mansion with no one for company but the servants and the Marquis, who is quite deaf and must needs be spoken to at the top of one's voice. I promise you *I* am quite exhausted after five minutes with him!"

Harriet hid a smile. Her aunt was looking quite chagrined. After all she had said about the Burbridges and their grand connections, she could scarce object now to their introducing Edward, not when he was practically related to Lady Burbridge.

There was no mistake about Sophy's reaction. Her eyes were shining with happiness, the pink of her cheeks just a fraction deeper, as she acknowledged the introduction, blushing a little as she admitted that Captain Danvers was already known to her. Lady Burbridge looked surprised, and then amused. So her young friend and Miss Wyclyffe were *épris!* How charming!

Fortunately, before she could give voice to these sentiments, someone else claimed her attention. For a moment Lady Phoebe glared at her daughter, until Philip, astutely summing up the situation, drew her attention to an acquaintance he wanted her to meet. While mourning the loss of Philip's company—he had scarcely addressed a word to her in the carriage and passed no comment on her gown, a circumstance which made Harriet feel very desolate indeed—she could not help being glad, for Sophy's sake, that he had intervened, although what Lady Phoebe would have to say to her daughter once they returned to South Audley Street, she shuddered to think!

Come to think of it, Harriet mused as she watched the endless parade of human life in front of her, Philip had been strangely morose, almost from the day they arrived in London. He no longer teased them, nor joked in his old fashion. She was worrying over his odd behavior when she became aware of a conversation being undertaken in low undertones slightly to her right.

While not wishing to eavesdrop, she could not, without making herself conspicuous, move out of earshot. The gentlemen were discussing the increasing number of French spies infiltrating the country, a subject which they obviously found very grave indeed. In direct contrast, on Harriet's other side, two ladies were chattering busily about the iniquitous price of French silk.

"Have you seen that gown Lady Mary is wearing?" one asked the other.

"Gown? I thought it was her shift!" exclaimed the other, with scarcely concealed chagrin. "She is quite brazen. Have you seen who she is with?"

"De la Valle, is it? It is all over town that she has taken up with him, but my dear, do you wonder at it? He is reputed to have a vast fortune, and we all know how fascinating she will find that!"

"Oh, indeed," her companion tittered angrily. "She quite ruined my sister's son, you know. Not that he had more than a feather to fly with, anyway. Butley had her in keeping at the time, but she soon left *him* when the Comte came on the scene!"

Shivering, Harriet moved out of the way. The venomous words lingered in her mind long after the women had gone, tiny drips of acid eating into her heart and making it burn with pain. She could not forget the way Philip had looked at Lady Mary, and she believed she understood now why he had been looking so preoccupied. As for the man who had bought her, like an expensive plaything! Harriet's eyes flashed. Of the two he was the worse, most definitely!

At that moment Lady Burbridge tapped her on the arm, exclaiming happily, "Ah, Miss Willoughby, I have been looking for you. Allow me to introduce you to the Comte de la Valle!"

Her normal shyness forgotten in the wave of anger that struck her on Philip's behalf, Harriet swung around, contempt and disdain only too plainly discernible in her normally warm eyes. She longed to say something extremely cutting, but respect for Lady Burbridge would not permit this breach of etiquette while she was enjoying her hospitality. Instead she contented herself with looking down her nose and proffering a rather limp hand. To her shocked dismay, instead of merely touching it, the Comte took her fingers and lifted them to his lips, pressing them against their warmth.

Confused, Harriet abandoned her pose, her eyes flying to the Comte's. Him! She choked back an unsteady gasp, unaware that she had gone paper white, or that her eyes had widened and remained fixed on the Comte's bored face.

"Charles, I have heard that you have a devastating effect upon my sex, but you appear to have completely bemused Miss Willoughby!" Only then did Harriet realize that Lady Mary was clinging to the Comte's arm, her red hair even more seductive at close quarters, eyes as green as jade surveying Harriet with amused contempt.

Blushing furiously, Harriet sought to disentangle herself. "Forgive me . . ." she said jerkily, "but . . ."

"But you were overcome with the heat," Lady Burbridge said, kindly coming to her rescue. "I know how it is, these rooms are like a hothouse." Dexterously she smoothed over the awkward moment, giving Harriet a reassuring smile and sending a servant to procure a glass of water for her. She watched Harriet drink it with sudden, jerky movements and asked kindly, "Do you feel better now?"

"Yes, thank you!" Harriet blushed again, biting her lip. "I thought I had seen the Comte before. He reminded me of someone."

"I know just how it is," Lady Burbridge agreed kindly. "It is a shock when one sees a stranger wearing a familiar face, but I am surprised you know someone with a likeness to Charles, for his looks are not commonplace!"

That was an understatement if ever there was one, Harriet thought weakly. The Comte was one of the most arresting gentlemen she had ever seen. She was sure not many men possessed just that aura of haughty indifference, nor the studied languid air, so much at variance with the only other man she knew with just exactly that olive-tinged skin and those strange gray eyes. She shivered suddenly with reaction, pressing anguished hands to her temples. It could not be true. She must be going mad. The Comte de la Valle, Lady Burbridge's august guest, a leading member of the Bourbon faction, and a French aristocrat, could not be the smuggler she had last seen wearing old ragged clothes and talking with a noticeable Sussex burr.

Over the heads of the other guests, Harriet snatched another feverish look at the Comte. He was talking to Lady Mary, plainly quite unconcerned with anything other than whatever they were discussing. He looked relaxed, even bored, his handsome, arrogant face set in lines of indolent amusement. He could *not* be the smuggler. Her imagination must be playing tricks on her. Why on earth would the Comte de la Valle want to masquerade as a common smuggler?

It was as though a cold hand had touched Harriet's heart. All too clearly she recalled the discussion she had overheard earlier; the gentlemen's concern over the number of French spies entering the country; the fact that Lord Burbridge was a prominent member of the Foreign

Office, likely to have access to all manner of secret documents.

I am imagining things, Harriet thought weakly. It is the shock of seeing someone who resembles the smuggler so closely, in such an unexpected fashion. Why, I dare say if I ever saw him again, I would find him quite different from the Comte. Nervously Harriet searched the ballroom. If she could just reassure herself that she was mistaken! She *must* reassure herself, she admitted with a tiny spurt of fear, otherwise she would be failing in her duty to her country. Allowing a smuggler to escape without reporting his crime was one thing. Keeping silent on a matter of national importance was another. Somehow she must convince herself that the Comte and the smuggler were two different people. She must devise a test for him, Harriet decided, a trap into which only a guilty man would fall. But how? She cudgelled her brain, her heart beating like a frightened doe's.

I must ask him if we have not met before, she told herself at length. If he denies it too strenuously, I shall know he is lying. Papa says a man cannot lie and look you in the eye at the same time. To make the decision was one thing, to carry it out quite another. Screwing up her courage, Harriet went in search of the Comte, her cheeks burning with shame as she remembered Lady Mary's derisory laughter. Discovering the truth was more important than any personal considerations, she told herself courageously.

Nervous and breathless, Harriet ran the Comte to earth by the french windows that looked out onto the narrow garden. Silently rehearsing her words, she approached him with a good deal of trepidation, which his bland acceptance of her stammered apology for disturbing him did little to lessen. "I expect Lady Burbridge has told you that I was overcome . . . by the heat . . ." Harriet offered a little falteringly, hating the lie.

The Comte seemed engrossed in removing a minute speck of dust from his immaculate coat, and he merely raised his black eyebrows a trifle and exclaimed laconically, "I trust you are recovered?"

Scarcely an auspicious start, but Harriet was determined to persevere. Taking a deep breath to steady herself, she said firmly, "Yes indeed. Tell me, Comte, have we not met before?"

Aware of the importance of watching her quarry's eyes, Harriet had nevertheless forgotten that the Comte was so very much taller than herself and was therefore obliged to tilt her face upwards toward his.

"I do not think so," he mused indifferently. "I am sure I should remember it if we had," he added as an afterthought, for all the world as though he were throwing a bone to a dog, Harriet thought, on a fresh wave of indignation. And as for watching his eyes! Since he was regarding her with a mocking insolence far more effective than her own fierce stare, it was she who was obliged to retreat in some disorder, dropping her lashes in blushing confusion as he drawled, "Forgive me, Miss . . . er . . . Willoughby, but are you short-sighted?"

Furious and tongue-tied, Harriet could only shake her head, but as she watched him walk away she reflected that the encounter had not been totally without reward. Now that she had had the opportunity to observe him again and at such close quarters, she was firmly convinced that the smuggler and the Comte *were* the same person, no matter how far-fetched it seemed.

It was a pity that there was no one who could corroborate the fact, and Harriet wondered if Edward Danvers knew that not twenty paces away from him was one of the very men he had so lately been hunting down. There was nothing else for it, Harriet thought determinedly. If there was no one she could turn to for aid, then she would have to unmask the Comte herself! The thought was both frightening and exhilarating.

It was a very thoughtful young lady who accompanied her cousins and aunt back to South Audley Street later that night. Who could have imagined, Harriet thought as she prepared for bed, that a French spy would be rash enough to parade himself openly before his greatest enemies. Pride goes before a fall, Harriet reflected in grim satisfaction, and she was going to make sure that the Comte's fall was an exceedingly hard one indeed!

chapter six

"Only think of it! Edward being related to Lady Burbridge—well, nearly related," Sophy allowed after a moment's judicious thought. "Even Mama cannot disapprove of him now!"

Privately Harriet thought her cousin too sanguine. There had been nothing in Lady Phoebe's attitude to suggest that she had in any way relented toward the Captain, but she was too fond of Sophy to dash her hopes by pointing out this fact.

In fact Sophy was finding her cousin unusually preoccupied. Harriet had more important matters on her mind than Sophy's love affair. Since quitting Lady Burbridge's home she had given a great deal of thought to the Comte de la Valle and the strange circumstances surrounding his double identity, and while she was more convinced than ever that he must be exposed in his true colors, she was still no nearer to deciding how best this admirable plan might be accomplished.

In other times she might have enlisted Philip's aid, Harriet mused, but they seldom saw him in South Audley Street these days. Philip had concerns other than the claims of his family to weigh upon him.

No, she would have to accomplish the task singlehanded!

These thoughts were disrupted by Sophy, who, growing bored with Harriet's absorption, declared impatiently, "Honestly, Harriet, I don't know what's the matter with you these days. You weren't listening to a word I was saying!"

A little guiltily Harriet denied this accusation.

"Very well, then," Sophy asked, artlessly, "will you come?"

"Come? Where?"

"So, I was right! I was just telling you, Harriet. I have arranged to meet Edward at Hatchards bookshop. You know Mama is forever saying I should improve my mind!" She pulled a face. "It would be better if you were to accompany me, though, otherwise Mama might suspect!"

Agreeing rather drily that nothing was more certain, Harriet obediently listened while Sophy poured out her plans. "Mama will think nothing of it if you come with me, Harriet," she coaxed. "Why, at home you always had your nose in a book!"

Unwilling to lend her aid to any plan that entailed deceiving her aunt, but unable to think of any good reason to refuse, Harriet was at last reluctantly persuaded to go upstairs for her pelisse so that she might accompany Sophy to her rendezvous.

"After all," Sophy said artlessly, once they were outside, "there is nothing improper about sitting in one of the reading rooms and drinking hot chocolate!"

"Nothing indeed," agreed Harriet, but she could not feel entirely easy about the venture. However, as they approached Hatchards, it occurred to her that Edward Danvers might just possibly be able to give her a little more insight into the character of the Comte, and so resolving to question him as discreetly as she could, Harriet agreed with her cousin's gay observation that in the case of Lady Phoebe it was most definitely a matter of what the eye did not see!

Fortunately Captain Danvers was waiting for them, supposedly engrossed in the *Morning Post,* which he dropped with flattering alacrity as he caught sight of the girls. Correctly interpreting the look Sophy gave her, Harriet expressed a desire to inspect the contents of the shelves a little more closely and left the two young lovers together, soothing her conscience with the thought that nothing untoward could pass between them in broad daylight in Hatchards, even had not Captain Danvers been a very proper and correct gentleman whose attentions to her cousin were quite obviously most respectable.

Having exhausted the authors A to F, Harriet decided it was time to return to Sophy. Captain Danvers welcomed her with a warm smile and ordered chocolate for them with much the gay air of a man ordering the very best wine, fit for a celebration. Whilst Sophy chattered enthusiastically about the elegant persons thronging the bookshop, Harriet took advantage of her absorption to question the Captain about the Comte.

From the quizzical look he gave her when she rather hesitantly raised the matter, Harriet guessed that her air of casual disinterest had not deceived Edward for one moment, and she flushed a little as she realized that some of his amusement was because he thought she was *romantically* interested in the Comte!

"A handsome enough gentleman, and very popular with the ladies," Edward informed her, adding a little cautiously, "Of course *I* do not know him personally, but I understand Lord Burbridge is very impressed with him." He saw Harriet's face droop a little, and mistaking the cause of her disappointment, said kindly, "The Comte tends to confine his attentions to married ladies, Miss Harriet. I collect that, unlike myself, he has an aversion to the state of marriage!" He squeezed Sophy's hand when he said this and gazed at her in a manner so affecting that Harriet was obliged to swallow the large lump which somehow had managed to lodge in her throat.

Plainly the Captain could not add to her pitifully small store of knowledge about the

Comte. She squared her shoulders. Very well, then! She would just have to rely upon her own ingenuity!

Absorbed in his Sophy, Edward Danvers barely noticed Harriet's determined expression. During his short stay in London he had heard a good deal more about the Comte than he had told Harriet. (His silence was mainly because of the fact that very little of the gossip flying about the town was to the Comte's credit, nor was it fit for repetition in the tender ears of a sheltered young lady, since it dealt almost entirely with the Comte's reputation as a lover and the speculation running rife as to whether Lady Mary would last any longer than the numerous other women in his life. One wit had already murmured that in the case of de la Valle and Lady Mary, it was not a matter of the hawk and the dove, but of the hawk and the vulture!—an unkind statement which, like so many unpleasantries, held a kernel of truth, certainly enough to make Lady Mary's green eyes flash when she heard it. Different from the gentler members of her sex in so many respects, she was still woman enough to dislike being likened to a flesh-eating vulture.)

If anything, Harriet was even more subdued when she accompanied Sophy back to South Audley Street, while the other girl was flushed and bubbling with happiness after her stolen half-hour with her lover. For Sophy's sake Harriet hoped she would contain her joy in her mama's presence, for she did not believe her eagle-eyed aunt would be deceived for one moment that it was merely the purchase of the latest "Gothic" romance that brought the color blooming to her daughter's cheeks.

Harriet's mood would not have been improved had she been privileged to see Philip. He was sitting in Brook's staring moodily into a glass of wine, oblivious to his surroundings. Only that morning he had seen Lady Mary walking down Bond Street on the arm of the Comte, both of them unaware of his presence. Philip had enough intelligence to see the folly of his infatuation, but sense and love seldom go hand in hand. While his head told him that he was making a laughing stock of himself, mooning about after a woman who was barely aware that he existed, his heart had only to recollect Lady Mary's undeniably lovely countenance to begin beating in a wildly erratic fashion, loud enough to drown out all the warnings of his mind.

That Lady Mary was the talk of the clubs he knew, but it made no difference. His infatuation was such that nothing could shake it. Already several of his friends, anxious on his behalf, had pointed out to him the dangers of the waters in which he was swimming. All to no avail. Coldly he told them that if they could say nothing good about the lady, they were to say nothing at all. Recognizing the violence of his affliction, they shrugged their shoulders and talked of other things, comforting themselves with the platitude that such ardor could only be short-lived and was best left to run its own course. Philip was as furiously resentful of their understanding silence as he had been of their mild criticism, and recognizing that he was fit company for neither man nor beast, he had taken to a more solitary existence than had previously been his wont.

The friendship between Lady Phoebe and Lady Burbridge continued to flourish, despite the setback of Lady Burbridge's connection with Captain Danvers, a fault which Lady Phoebe large-mindedly allowed was none of her friend's doing. A word in Lady Burbridge's ear, she decided calmly, would put matters to rights in that direction. She would be surely as anxious for her young friend to make a good marriage as Lady Phoebe was for Sophy, and the hint that Sophy had no expectations bar the very modest dowry her father could give her would be as beneficial to the young man as it would to Sophy.

An invitation for Lady Phoebe and her charges to take tea with Lady Burbridge and be introduced to Lady Sefton took Lady Phoebe's carriage through the Park en route to Cavendish Square. It was Harriet's loving eyes that spotted Philip first, her betraying gasp drawing Lady Phoebe's suspicious glance to her niece's vividly flushed face and thence through the carriage window to the carriageway where her son was riding at the side of Lady Mary, plainly unaware and uncaring of his mama's presence.

"Good Heavens, Mama! Look over there, Philip riding with Lady Mary!" exclaimed Sophy, guilelessly, adding ingenuously, "I thought she was the Comte de la Valle's friend!"

"Sophy!" warned her mama repressively, causing that young lady to subside against the cushions, wondering what she had said wrong.

As they alighted outside Lady Burbridge's, Sophy squeezed Harriet's fingers commiseratingly and whispered, "I should not worry, Harriet, all young men have these foolish notions about older women. Philip will grow out of it, I am sure!" Easy for her to say, Harriet thought bleakly, but would Sophy have felt as sanguine had it been Edward staring down so adoringly into the flamboyantly beautiful face raised enticingly to his?

Lady Sefton was very gracious, accepting Lady Phoebe's thanks for the coveted vouchers with a faint smile and a small inclination of her head as she murmured that she was sure two such charming young ladies as Miss Sophy and Miss Harriet could but add to Almacks' luster.

It was while her aunt was involved in a long, and to Harriet, extremely dull, recital of her antecedents and those of her niece that Lady Burbridge leaned across and asked Harriet if she would mind stepping into Lord Burbridge's study, which she would find off the main hall, and bringing her the diary she would find on the desk. By way of explanation, she informed her that she wanted to check the date of Prinny's Grand Ball to discover if whether there was still time to try to procure invitations for Lady Phoebe and the girls.

Harriet found the study easily enough. It had a heavy wooden door that was hard to open, and for a moment Harriet was dazzled as the sunlight streaming in through the tall windows blinded her. Shading her eyes, she had a first impression of bookcases flanking a marble fireplace, a large desk, and several comfortable chairs. Her second impression was that she was not alone in the room. Someone was standing by the desk, bending over an open drawer. One of the servants? Surely not, Harriet thought, her heart beating strangely fast, until the explanation occurred to her. Lord Burbridge's secretary, of course! She recollected Lady Burbridge saying that her husband dealt with such a large volume of work that he had found it necessary to engage a young man to help him undertake his many duties. Clearing her throat a little self-consciously, Harriet moved farther into the room.

The man standing by the desk straightened slowly, plainly in no hurry to discover the identity of the intruder. Harriet had a moment's disoriented impression of dark hair, burnished blue-black where the sunlight rested on it, a lithe, powerful frame, and sardonically cool eyes, as he folded his arms and stared at her.

"You!" Harriet choked, her betraying gaze flying to the open drawer. The Comte's mocking glance reminded her that this was the *second* time she had stared at him in such a fashion.

"What are you doing in Lord Burbridge's study?" she demanded.

"My dear young lady, I might ask you the same question," the Comte drawled, plainly enjoying himself. "What *are* you doing, by the way?"

Finding the initiative taken out of her hands in such a startling manner, Harriet could only stare at the Comte, trying to recover her scattered wits.

"I am come on an errand for Lady Burbridge," she told him loftily, "but you have still not explained your presence!"

The Comte dropped into one of Lord Burbridge's leather chairs, smiling a little quizzically into Harriet's stubbornly hostile face. "Come, child, surely there is no need for all this heat? What do you think I am doing, purloining the silver?" he suggested softly.

Harriet flushed at the mocking tone, but held her ground. "Hardly, for I am sure the *silver* is under lock and key in the butler's pantry."

"Ah. I see," drawled the Comte, getting to his feet and surveying her thoughtfully. "Let me see now, I collect you construe my motives for being here as most definitely of a base nature?" He stroked his chin, and Harriet could have sworn there was a gleam of amusement in his eyes. "So, if it is not the silver, then what can it be, I wonder?"

"Cease toying with me!" Harriet commanded, only just resisting the temptation to stamp her foot. "I know full well why you are here! You are a French spy," she told him roundly, "and I shall tell Lord Burbridge what I found you doing!"

Before she realized what he was doing, the Comte was behind her, firmly closing the door. He leaned against it, eyeing Harriet with a laconic contemplation that did nothing to steady her uneven heartbeats. She licked her lips a little nervously, and the Comte smiled as his eyes took in this betraying gesture.

"Not so brave now, eh, Miss Willoughby?" he said softly. "Do you really suppose if I were a spy, I should allow you to leave so readily? A very tame creature you must think me!"

Tame! Harriet shuddered. He was anything but that! Even leaning casually against the door, he had an aura of lean, coiled strength, like a tiger about to spring, Harriet thought, trembling.

"Are you trying to tell me you are *not* a spy?" she asked a little breathlessly, when she had her breath back.

"Do you find that so hard to believe?" The Comte parried. "I promise you I am nothing so dangerous!"

"Then what are you doing in here, rifling through Lord Burbridge's desk?" she shot back.

"Rifling? Oh, come, Miss Willoughby, surely that is a rather strong term? If you must have the truth, there is a perfectly simple explanation for my presence!"

He smiled, and again Harriet had the disturbing conviction that he was amused, rather than annoyed by her accusation. He was trying to catch her off guard, she told herself, her lip curling with disdain. Doubtless he was used to females practically swooning into his arms, and expected to charm her in much the same way as he had charmed Lady Mary! Gritting her teeth, Harriet vowed that that would not be so.

"I should be interested to hear that explanation, sir," she told him coldly. "but you had best be swift about it, for if I am gone much longer, Lady Burbridge will doubtless be coming to see what has delayed me!"

The Comte's eyes were uncomfortably perceptive. "Frightened, Miss Willoughby? You need not be, my dear, I never trifle with children, even such adorable, wrong-headed children as yourself! Now, where was I? Oh, yes, my explanation." He levered his shoulders off the door, and Harriet could only think, in a disjointed fashion, that the Comte was possessed of extremely broad shoulders and that the dark blue cloth of his coat set them off to distinct advantage. Philip could have told her that such a coat could only have come from the hands of a master tailor, such as the great Weston himself, and that the Comte's biscuit yellow pantaloons, which clung to powerful thighs, had come from the same source, and like the rest of the Comte's apparel had the stamp of a quality which only a good deal of money could buy. Naturally enough, since Harriet was not *au fait* with the intricacies of a gentleman's wardrobe, her bemused eyes only noticed that the Comte's cravat was tied in an extremely intricate fashion and that his Hessian boots had a shine in which she could see her own features reflected quite perfectly. Discomposed by the Comte's patent amusement, Harriet continued to stare downward, until he drawled, in a voice which she was sure held more than a suspicion of laughter, "Yes, my boots are very fine, aren't they? Hoby himself made them, and they were quite ruinously expensive, but you will not find the explanation you seek by staring at the floor, Miss Willoughby. It is really quite simple, you know, I was doing nothing more sinister than collecting some papers for Lord Burbridge."

Glaring at him, Harriet had it on the tip of her tongue to challenge this statement, and the

Comte must have read her mind with deadly accuracy, she thought later, for he added unmercifully, "You may ask him yourself, if you choose. I promise you he will be greatly entertained by the notion that you consider me a spy."

"Because in his kind-heartedness he is deceived in you!" Harriet retorted heatedly. "You can say what you will, Comte, but I *know* you for a liar and a cheat!"

Snatching up the diary, she was through the door before he could prevent her, her heart beating in her breast like a wild thing.

Fortunately, only Sophy appeared to have noticed the length of her absence, and she seemed quite happy with Harriet's whispered explanation that she had mistaken the room and had had to be redirected by one of the servants.

"I've never seen such a large house!" Sophy agreed under cover of their elders' conversation. "Although Edward says his grandfather's mansion is nearly twice as large, and their country seat more so!"

For several minutes she talked voluably of the Marquis's possessions, confiding to Harriet her hope that somehow or other the Marquis might be persuaded to do something for his grandson—a something that would persuade Lady Phoebe to give her consent to their marriage. Agreeing with Sophy that this would be the perfect solution to their problem, Harriet relived her ordeal in the study, trying to take a more dispassionate view of the Comte's conversation than she had been able to do at the time. There was no doubt that he was a formidable adversary, she acknowledged with a shiver. Somehow she found his scarcely concealed amusement more dangerous than anger, but she would best him yet, she told herself fiercely. She would prove to the world that he *was* a spy.

Unaware of her cousin's thoughts, Sophy chattered on happily about Edward and the idyllic future they would share if only her mama could be brought to see reason. She diverged from this delightful prospect only long enough to comment on Philip's growing attachment to Lady Mary. "That will give Mama something more to think about than Edward!" she told Harriet with satisfaction, belatedly aware of her cousin's stricken face.

"You don't mean that Philip would *marry* Lady Mary, do you?" Harriet whispered.

"Oh, heavens, no," Sophy assured her airily. "Lady Mary would not want to, for Philip is not rich, you know, but you know how Mama is with him." She pulled a wry face. "Poor Philip, this will bring him down off his pedestal with a vengeance. Mama is forever prosing on about his excellent character, and I wonder what she will find to say now that he has got himself into the clutches of such a notorious woman?"

"Perhaps it is no more than a brief infatuation," Harriet suggested in troubled accents.

"Oh, but of course," Sophy answered with a shrug, adding with a sophistication that surprised her more innocent cousin, "But then *they* are the most dangerous, and you know how moral Philip is. I wonder that he manages to reconcile Lady Mary's reputation with his own high standards, but I expect he is too far gone to care. Did you see the way he was looking at her? He is quite besotted, but I dare say the Comte will have something to say about Lady Mary going riding with him," Sophy added wisely, "and that will probably put an end to it, for she will never prefer Philip above the Comte."

Heartsore, Harriet was left to reflect on Sophy's words as they rode back to South Audley Street. Poor Philip, and poor her, she thought with an unusual touch of self-pity, what was there to say that Philip would ever turn to her, even if Lady Mary did cast him off? For some reason, the knowledge did not hurt as sharply as she had expected, and long after she had abandoned the subject of Philip, her mind was still busily toying with the best means of bringing that odious and totally reprehensible character, the Comte de la Valle, to justice. Having regained her bedchamber without a solution presenting itself to her, Harriet lay on her bed and stared at the ceiling, trying to disentangle her disordered thoughts.

That night was the occasion of their presentation at Almacks. Harriet found herself looking forward to the evening with less pleasure than she should have done. Philip was to accompany them, but when he presented himself, dressed in black satin breeches and evening pumps, his expression was so bitter that it immediately cast a cloud over Harriet's enjoyment.

She was wearing another of her new gowns, a pale green silk emphasizing her ethereal appearance, lustrous curls brushing her slender white shoulders as she hurried downstairs. A touch of color in her cheeks emphasized the depth and size of her eyes, and she was almost surprised when she glanced in the mirror and saw how her looks had improved since coming to London. A spangled shawl completed her toilette, and gathering her fan and reticule, she followed Sophy out to the waiting carriage.

They had both been warned that they would not be allowed to waltz until suitable partners were presented to them by one of the patronesses, and bearing this advice in mind, Harriet refused the flattering coaxing of a young gentleman in an ensign's uniform to stand up with her. The Honorable Toby was similarly engaged in soliciting Sophy's hand, but Lady Burbridge, kind-heartedly thinking to do the young people a favor, had prevailed upon Lady Sefton to present Edward Danvers to Sophy as a partner. Naturally enough, this did not find approval in Lady Phoebe's eyes, but since there was little she could do, she favored her daughter with an over-sweet smile and inclined her head in Edward's direction with arctic frostiness.

"We shall have to find a partner for you, Harriet," Lady Sefton was just saying when she broke off to stare at the double doors. "Good gracious, I do believe that is de la Valle!"

Harriet could find nothing astonishing in the Comte's presence and agreed rather indifferently that the gentleman entering did appear to have the Comte's arresting features.

"I don't believe he's been here on more than a couple of occasions since he arrived in London. I wonder what brings him tonight," Lady Sefton murmured, eyeing the newcomer with interest.

"Perhaps he is looking for Lady Mary," Harriet suggested without interest.

"Oh, no!" Lady Sefton replied, in such positive accents that both Lady Phoebe and Harriet stared at her. "The patronesses do not allow persons of Lady Mary's reputation to attend the dances," she announced by way of explanation.

"But that is so unfair," Harriet started to say rebelliously, before a glance from her aunt quelled her. She knew well enough that while a *gentleman's* aberrations were permitted, any deviation on the part of a woman from the path of virtue immediately resulted in her exclusion from the more exalted ranks of her own kind. She had heard her aunt talk disparagingly of "muslin company," and even Mama had told her hesitantly of the liaisons conducted by gentlemen with members of the opposite sex, which had nothing to do with the serious business of marriage and procreation of children. Bewildered by the unfairness of it all, Harriet subsided into silence, unaware that the Comte was advancing upon them, until she heard Lady Sefton exclaiming in plainly astonished accents, "Miss Willoughby? But of course, Comte. Harriet, my child, pray allow me to present the Comte to you. I promise you he waltzes extremely well!"

Taking this comment to mean that Lady Sefton was giving her permission to dance with the Comte, Harriet glanced first at her aunt, and finding no help there, risked an upward glance at the gentleman towering above her. "Perhaps you do not waltz, Miss Willoughby?" he asked so patronizingly that Harriet was denying his assertion before she realized how neatly he had trapped her.

Two minutes later, circling the floor in his admittedly firm arms, Harriet her face determinedly averted, refused to acknowledge her partner by so much as a flicker of an eyelash, until the Comte murmured dulcetly, "You would enjoy the dance far more and perform it more gracefully if you would just relax a little, my child, otherwise the whole world will know that you have never danced so close to a man before." Not knowing how seriously to take him, Harriet almost stumbled and felt his arm tighten about her waist as he made use of her inattention to draw her closer to him.

She had known he was tall, Harriet thought, but not that the top of her own head would barely reach his chin, and surely there was no need for him to rest his jaw against her ringlets when he drew her into the turn? She glanced upward and found him regarding her with amusement.

"What thoughts lurk in that suspicious little heart of yours, I wonder, Miss Willoughby? Still planning my downfall, are you?" He laughed against her ear, and Harriet shivered suddenly. "You will not win, my child, the fight is an unequal one, and you had best abandon it now."

"By saying as much, you are admitting that there is a need to fight," Harriet told him. "I would be failing in my duty to my country if I did not unmask you."

"Has it struck you, I wonder," the Comte asked a little drily, "that if I were a spy, you would be in the utmost danger?"

It had occurred to her, and she trembled a little, refusing to back down. "As to that, you could hardly do away with me . . . not without betraying yourself, at least!"

"How naive," she heard the Comte murmur, "and I suppose you would even be prepared to make that sacrifice if you thought it would serve your purpose? I wonder if you realize how very young you are?"

"I realize that you are trying to lull my suspicions by mocking me and treating me like a child," Harriet retorted with a touch of asperity, "but you will not succeed!"

"So I am beginning to perceive," agreed the Comte with a touch of humor. "You have perseverance, if nothing else. So, it is to be war between us, is it?"

"It is war between our two countries," Harriet pointed out, "and you would not expect me to make a friend of my country's enemy, especially when I know him to be deceitful."

"Ah, how moral you are," mocked the Comte. "You would be hard to live with, my child, that uncomfortable conscience of yours forever obtruding itself. Come, give me a smile, for I see Lady Sefton is watching us. She will warn you that I am a sad rake and not to be taken seriously by such a young and innocent child, but then I have never deceived you, have I?"

"Never!" Harriet answered spiritedly as the music stopped. "Lady Sefton has no need to warn me against *you!*"

He laughed, and his laughter rang in Harriet's ears long after she was warm and safe in her bed wondering how best she might defeat him. For once, her normally acute perceptions, where Philip was concerned, were in abeyance.

She had not seen her cousin leaving Almacks, a fixed expression on his face as he curtly refused a hackney and started to walk determinedly through the silent streets.

His goal was the small house in Mayfair occupied by Lady Mary. Toby had informed him that the house had been bought and paid for with the Comte's money, but Philip refused to listen, just as he refused to acknowledge the fact that the Comte was Lady Mary's protector. Like many a besotted youth before him, he refused to see his goddess as anything but misunderstood, a waif in the storm, battered by cruel fate and only in need of a safe harbor to show herself in her true light. It had never occurred to him that Lady Mary was content with her lot, that she actually preferred her present life to that of a respectable wife.

A small giggling maid opened the door to Philip's knock. Upstairs Lady Mary heard him give his name and smiled to herself. She was not in the best of moods. She had waited all night for Charles and had not been best pleased to learn that instead of visiting her he had taken himself off to Almacks! Almacks, of all places, that insipid haunt of virtuous gossips and half-grown children. She hunched a petulant white shoulder against a silk cushion, uncaring that her negligee had slipped to reveal the seductively full curve of her breast. It was time she taught Master Charles a lesson. When the girl entered with the information that there was a young gentleman asking for her downstairs, she was ready.

"Pray desire him to step upstairs, Betty," she drawled, without batting an eyelid, "and Betty . . ."

"Yes, madam."

"We are not to be disturbed. Do you understand?"

A long look passed between mistress and maid.

"Yes, miss."

"Very well. You may send the gentleman up."

Bemused, Philip found himself shown into, not a sitting room as he had expected, but what was very obviously Lady Mary's bedchamber, with Lady Mary herself reclining very much at her ease on a green satin daybed that exactly matched the color of her eyes. Indeed, it was quite surprising that Philip should notice this fact at all, since Lady Mary was clad in a wispy veiling of green chiffon which did more to reveal than conceal her admittedly desirable curves.

Hastily averting his eyes from the spectacle of so much delectable milk-white flesh, Philip stammered a greeting and was commanded to sit down and make himself at home. Since the room possessed nothing to sit on save the sofa and an extremely large bed, Philip looked about him with a rather hunted look until Lady Mary swung her long legs off the sofa and patted the space beside her.

The smile she turned on Philip held all the promise of Lilith herself, and he would have to have been made of stone to resist the enchantment of it and the insidious clamor of his own senses. With Lady Mary's moist lips parting beneath his own, he forgot everything save the sweet torment of the moment and the heady pleasure of the languorous body beneath his own.

Only a soft laugh in his ear reminded him that he might have been a trifle importunate, but since the lady offered no further protest, Philip smothered the qualms of his conscience and submitted to the exquisite pleasure of having Lady Mary in his arms.

Neither of them heard the soft click as the doorhandle turned nor the maid's feeble gasp as the Comte pushed her firmly to one side and entered the room. The first Philip knew of his presence was when he heard him drawling unpleasantly, "A pretty scene, indeed, madam. Is this, then, how you entertain yourself when I am not here?"

His disparaging glance swept Philip's embarrassed face and rested fleetingly on Lady Mary's voluptuous body. Picking up a wrap from the bed, he tossed it to her saying casually, "Put this on. My poor Mary, have I neglected you so badly, then, that you are reduced to robbing the cradle?"

Philip could not believe his ears. Was the Comte not even going to challenge him? Apparently not, he deduced as the Frenchman continued to ignore him. His earlier ardor waned a little as he saw the way in which Lady Mary was regarding her protector, plainly quite unembarrassed at being thus surprised. Was that all he meant to her, Philip asked himself bitterly, a momentary diversion, nothing more?

"I suggest you leave, Wyclyffe," the Comte drawled without taking his eyes off Lady Mary. "That soft-hearted cousin of yours will be anxious for you."

Philip didn't pause to wonder how the Comte had gained such an intimate knowledge of Harriet that he was able to describe her as "soft-hearted." As his feet clattered down the stairs, all he could think of was Lady Mary, and the mocking look she had thrown him when the Comte dismissed him. Was he a mere boy that he should so meekly have done the Frenchman's bidding, he asked himself when he was out on the street? But there was nothing to be gained by going back now, and besides, he told himself fiercely, no gentleman would argue over a lady in that same lady's presence. Heartsore at Lady Mary's cavalier treatment, he wandered back to Half Moon Street.

The Comte surveyed his mistress through half-closed eyes. Lady Mary pouted.

"Come, Charles, you are not really cross, are you? A boy, nothing more!"

"Then why torment him?" asked the Comte negligently. "Or was I supposed to be the victim?"

Lady Mary shrugged her shoulders. She was far too astute to be betrayed into an admission of jealousy. "I thought he might be useful to us. They say he has a good future in Government circles; who knows what services he might be able to do us?"

"But that," the Comte told her firmly, leaning down to remove her wrapper, "is for the future, and for now, I am only concerned with the present."

"I thought you would be pleased, Charles," Lady Mary murmured huskily, twining her arms about his neck, "but it doesn't matter. He is a boy and amusing, but you are a man."

His slightly cynical smile seemed to convey agreement. Certainly when the maid tiptoed upstairs to listen at the door, there was nothing to suggest that the matter had not been settled most amicably.

chapter seven

To Lady Phoebe's great joy, Lady Burbridge had managed to procure invitations for them to attend the Regent's Ball. Not, unfortunately, at the same table as Lord Burbridge and herself—they were to sit with the French contingent at the top table—but nevertheless, Lady Phoebe could count herself very lucky indeed to be attending. As she reminded both girls nigh on half a dozen times a day, it would be a great thing to tell their grandchildren when they were old and gray, that they had dined with the Prince Regent.

Naturally, such an important event called for new gowns, and an urgent letter to Sir George brought a draft drawn on his bankers, Messrs. Hoares, which Philip was to cash for his mama

122

to enable her to meet this additional expense. Sir George had been generous, and this time there was no talk of Grafton House. Instead, some frighteningly expensive material had been purchased from Leyton & Shears, under Lady Burbridge's guidance. She warned Lady Phoebe that since the dining room was to be decorated all in the Bourbon colors with one anteroom hung with blue velvet embellished with ermine fleur de lys, it would be wise to choose colors that would not clash with this display. Lady Burbridge also told them that the Prince had designed new uniforms for his household, especially for the occasion. "The most dreadful peacocking colors, I promise you. Poor Burbridge declares they will all look worse than a bunch of corsair pirates!"

As a foil for Prinny's décor Lady Phoebe had declared that they would all wear blue, a safe color, becoming to any lady, young or old. She herself had elected to wear a majestic blue velvet with Sophy in palest blue muslin and Harriet in a misty mixture more mauve-gray than strictly blue, but infinitely becoming to her coloring. Sophy pouted a little when she saw it, declaring that it was far prettier than *her* gown, but as Fitch soothingly pointed out, Sophy would be one of the few girls present to wear a gown so exactly matching the color of her eyes.

Philip, duly presenting himself at South Audley Street to escort his ladies, wore regulation evening clothes, being neither a member of Prinny's household nor able to sport any regimentals. Sophy teased him, saying that he looked like a black crow, but Harriet's perceptive eyes saw his faintly haggard expression and the bitterness he could not quite conceal when he thought no one was observing him, and her heart sank.

Carlton House was ablaze with lights when they eventually arrived, the atmosphere inside so oppressive that Harriet found she could hardly breathe. The Prince had a terror of illness, another sympathetic lady murmured to her as she saw her expression, and kept huge fires burning in every room lest he take a chill. Privately, Harriet thought the excessive heat more unhealthy than any cool fresh air, but refrained from saying as much.

They were shown into an enormous gallery laid out with tables covered in plate and porcelain, an artificial stream winding its way down the tables, live gold and silver fish shimmering in the light from the enormous chandeliers.

Harriet had never seen anything like it before in her life. Lady Burbridge had told them that the Prince had spent a fortune on the house, and she could well believe it, although for her own tastes everything was too opulent, too rich; she felt that after several hours in one of the rooms, one would feel slightly sick, with a nausea similar to the aftermath of too many rich sweets.

On the way to the gallery they had already seen the anteroom hung with the Bourbon arms, where the Prince had received Louis. Now it was crowded with members of the *ton*, and as she took her place at the table Harriet had her first glimpse of "Prinny" himself, resplendent in one of his ornate uniforms, the glitter of the orders upon his chest out-dazzling the jewels of the woman seated on his left.

Lady Burbridge had pulled a wry face when she told them that Lady Hertford was to act as the Prince's hostess. Although it was not "done" to say so, she felt that it was a great shame that Maria Fitzherbert's restraining influence had ever been removed. Naturally no one mentioned the secret marriage the Prince was supposed to have contracted with his paramour, but Harriet's tender heart ached for the lady, who, many said, had been a better wife to the Regent than anyone else could be.

Naturally enough, since Edward was not present, Sophy could find little to please her in the occasion, although she did urge Harriet rather loudly to "only look and see who is seated opposite the Comte."

Dutifully complying with this command, Harriet raised her head and glanced toward the top table, hurriedly looking away again as she perceived that the Comte was watching *her* with mocking intent.

"Did you see Lady Mary?" Sophy hissed.

Harriet had barely noticed her, but she saw Philip pale and push his food away as though suddenly unable to touch it. He drank his wine, though—more than Harriet thought wise, as she watched the liveried footmen constantly filling the glasses. Poor Philip, did he hope that the wine would somehow lessen the ache of his longing for Lady Mary?

It was not merely his longing that Philip was having to contend with. A long, sober look at himself in his shaving mirror that morning had reassured him that he had not changed into some monster of depravity, but nothing could quite quell the feeling of repugnance that had dogged him since that moment in Lady Mary's bedchamber. He had always considered himself a man of honor, rigidly adhering to the same code as had his father and his grandfather before him, and yet he had stolen from another man, just as guiltily as though he had put his hand in his pocket and removed his purse. Lady Mary lived in a house provided for her by the Comte, and she made no secret of the fact that he bought her clothes, provided her carriage, and even paid her gambling debts, Philip admitted unhappily, and that made her as much the Frenchman's possession as though he had bought her in the marketplace. Philip could not believe the lady had allowed it to happen willingly; the Comte must have some hold over her—a hold which Philip meant to break, and thereby free Lady Mary to be the sweet, loving creature he was sure she really was.

When the clashing of the trumpets, which accompanied every course, had finally died away and the tables were removed, Lord Burbridge sent his secretary across to make sure they were quite comfortable—a circumstance which, Lady Phoebe complacently advised her neighbor, was only what might be expected of a gentleman of Lord Burbridge's breeding.

Mr. Thomas Fiennes was every bit as efficient and capable as one might have expected of anyone connected with Lord Burbridge's household, and in the twinkling of an eye he had procured chairs for them and diverted a flunkey bearing a tray of wineglasses.

Harriet smiled at Mr. Fiennes as she accepted her glass, albeit a little reluctantly, for she was still no fonder of the stuff. Although well-born, Mr. Fiennes came of an impoverished family who had had the misfortune to support the Stuart cause. After the debacle of Culloden, they had been stripped of rank and wealth as an example to anyone foolish enough to continue to support the "Pretender." Both Harriet and Sophy had thought it a sad tale and felt for the young man who would only be able to make his way in the world on the recommendation of others, although Lady Phoebe, less sentimental, considered the young gentleman to be very fortunate indeed. As Lord Burbridge's protégé he was bound to go far!

Harriet looked longingly toward the closed french windows. She would love a breath of fresh air, and wondered how the gentlemen felt in their heavy uniforms. Seeing that Lady Phoebe was deep in conversation and that Sophy was still chattering to Mr. Fiennes, she slipped quietly away. The gardens were virtually deserted. The faint tinkle of a fountain drew her. It was a clear night, with stars shining as brightly as the ladies' diamonds at the dinner table, and she drew a deep breath of fresh air, savoring the cool breeze on her heated cheeks.

A glance into the drawing room assured her that Lady Phoebe was still deep in conversation. Adjusting her silver-fringed shawl, Harriet wandered deeper into the coolness of the gardens. The scent of roses lay heavily on the evening air, somehow much more disturbingly potent than during the daytime, when their beauty distracted the senses away from their perfume. Harriet was about to pluck one when a figure detached itself from the shadows, the splendor of one of "Prinny's" uniforms unmistakable despite the darkness.

As the gentleman lurched toward her, Harriet realized that he had had rather too much to drink. Holding her head up, she smiled bravely, wishing she had not wandered quite so far from the safety of the well-lit french windows. The gentleman was near enough for Harriet to smell the wine on his breath. Clutching her shawl about her, she stepped back, suppressing a start as she realized that the pergola about which the roses twined cut off her retreat. Telling herself that there was nothing to fear, Harriet bade him a good evening and made to walk past. "Leaving so soon, fair one?" the gentleman drawled, slurring his words a little. "Come, a kiss for me before you go, eh?"

Harriet told herself that he did not mean to be offensive, but nevertheless she was trembling a little, shocked by the blatant desire that even her innocence recognized. Too late she recalled the tales Edward had told them about the raffish and sometimes dissolute gentlemen who surrounded the Prince. Coarse fingers gripped her chin, and a shaft of moonlight showed her the heavy features of a man who had indulged too freely in the pleasures of life.

"Just one kiss," he coaxed, his body blocking Harriet's escape, "just one kiss, and you can have your freedom!"

It was no one's fault but her own that she was being subjected to such insulting behavior, Harriet told herself. She should never have ventured unattended into the gardens in the first place. She bit her lip trying to stem the threatening tears, glancing helplessly toward the french windows, praying that Philip or Sophy would notice her disappearance and come searching for her. She closed her eyes as her persecutor's face swam nearer, her ears suddenly catching the faint sounds of firm footsteps along the gravel. Opening her eyes, she saw the familiar plain black of Philip's evening dress as he advanced toward them. Her assailant gave a sharp oath as he was plucked from her. Almost fainting with relief, Harriet heard a faint splash as her rescuer deposited him into the ornamental pool she had been admiring only minutes before.

Thank goodness! Her prayer had been answered after all. Hurrying toward the pool, she flung herself into Philip's arms with a choked cry, "Philip, please don't be cross. That horrid man!" She shuddered convulsively, glad of Philip's protective arms as they closed about her. "He was quite dreadfully drunk!"

"Most reprehensible!" drawled a voice against Harriet's ear, turning her blood to ice. "Unfortunately, Miss Willoughby, I am not Philip. I conjecture you have made yet another of those lamentable 'mistakes.' If you will just look through yonder window, you will see your cousin dancing with Lady Mary!"

Crimson with mortification, Harriet froze. She felt ready to sink with embarrassment. How could she have been foolish enough to mistake the Comte for Philip! If she had not been so terrified, no doubt she would never have been so stupid, but it would be difficult to convince the Comte—who, she could see, was regarding her with every evidence of amusement—she reflected bitterly, trying to withdraw herself from his arms, arms which somehow or other appeared to have tightened about her without any apparent effort on the Comte's part!

"If you will just release me," Harriet said unsteadily, "I shall return to my aunt."

"What? Is that all you can say?" taunted the Comte. "No threats to unmask me? No aspersions cast upon my character? You disappoint me, Miss Willoughby. Am I to suppose that you have at last come to your senses?"

Stung by his mockery, Harriet glared up at him. "No such thing," she said defiantly. "I know you to be a spy, Comte, no matter how much you may try to convince me to the contrary, and I shall not rest until you are unmasked!"

Harriet gasped as his fingers dug into her shoulders, his face tightening with anger, as he shook her. "I suppose one must excuse the foolishness of a child who knows no better, but I warn you, Miss Willoughby, you are dabbling in matters of which you know naught. Be careful lest you get hurt," he warned her grimly.

"Are you threatening me, Comte?" Harriet asked bravely. "For all that you call me a child, I am old enough to see through *you!*"

"Are you so?" gritted the Comte with the air of a man suddenly come to the end of his patience. "So, it is to be war between us, then, is it? Let us hope the victory is not a Pyrrhic one!"

"It will not be, for me," Harriet told him firmly, trying to disengage herself from his arms. "And please remove your hands. It is unnecessary for you to hold me so now, I am quite safe!"

"Are you so?" drawled the Comte sardonically. "I hate to destroy such touching faith. What would you say, I wonder, if I were to claim the reward you were plainly ready to give young Wyclyffe."

"Philip is my cousin," Harriet retorted stiffly, trying to avoid the cool mockery of the Comte's gray eyes.

"Ah, but I think it was not merely cousinly consolation you sought in his arms, eh, Miss Willoughby, and I am as well able to supply your needs as any other man!"

"My needs?" Harriet stammered, not totally understanding the gleam in his eyes.

Above her she heard the Comte mutter something unintelligible, and then she was crushed against his chest, his fingers sliding through her ringlets and forcing her face upward toward his own. "*Dieu*, but you make a man lose all patience, Miss Willoughby," she heard him say in an oddly thick voice. "Are you really as innocent as you seem, or is it all just a mockery—an appealing mask worn to deceive the mere male like so many of your sex?"

Too bewildered to fully comprehend what he meant, Harriet murmured an incoherent protest at the fierceness of his hold upon her curls, her small fists pushing uselessly at his chest.

"Why are you doing this?" she asked piteously when he refused to release her.

"Why? Perhaps because you arouse the hunter in me, I do not know," he murmured against her lips, stifling her shaken protest with the pressure of his mouth.

Instantly Harriet was transported to that moment in Smugglers' Wood. The lips burning hers so passionately now were the same ones that had kissed her then—she knew it with every fiber of her being; with a knowledge as instinctive and irrefutable as that that told her the Comte represented a greater danger to her than anything she had ever experienced before.

The hand in her ringlets gradually relaxed its cruel hold, caressing where it had been tugging, the hard lips growing insistently demanding as they plundered the full sweetness of her own.

Somewhere deep inside her, Harriet felt a melting warmth that made her tremble with shock at its unexpectedness. She shuddered deeply and was instantly freed, the Comte breathing hard as he stepped back.

"Another time, you will not be so trusting," he said harshly as his eyes raked her with cold contempt.

Driven to protect herself, Harriet forced herself to hold his gaze. "Unwanted though your embrace was, sir, it has confirmed one thing!"

"And what is that, pray, that I am not a gentleman?"

"That I already knew," Harriet whipped back. "No, this is something more important."

Harriet had the impression that he was inspecting her, those penetrating eyes missing nothing, from the nervous way she clasped her hands together to the irregular beat of her heart.

"Perhaps you will enlighten me? I own I am coming to expect, if not the unorthodox, then certainly the unusual from those soft lips of yours."

The abrupt change from anger to laconic mockery startled Harriet. The Comte was leaning negligently against a pillar, seemingly quite at ease, a small smile curving his mouth. It was hard to reconcile him with the man who had said her name so harshly only a few minutes ago, and who had kissed her as though he almost hated her.

"Well?" he prompted softly. "Or do you intend to keep me in suspense?"

Harriet shrugged, trying to match his own careless insouciance. "'Tis merely this, sir. Before, I might have owned that there was a chance I could have been mistaken in you—"

"I am relieved to hear it," the Comte drawled.

"But now," Harriet continued, as though he had not spoken, "I know that I was not!"

"Ah!" The Comte lounged back, studying her thoughtfully. "And are you going to tell me why?"

"Harriet? Where are you? Mama is asking for you!"

"Sophy!" Harriet said involuntarily, turning in the direction of her cousin's voice.

The Comte frowned. "Unfortunate! I do not think it would be wise for us to be discovered thus, Miss Willoughby. Your cousin is something of a chatterbox, and I should hate young Wy-clyffe to feel honor bound to call me out for ruining your reputation, although from an ethical point of view it should prove an interesting point," he murmured drily, smiling mockingly at Harriet's expression. "Nothing for you to worry your pretty head about, my child. A matter between your cousin and myself. You had best leave now before your cousin finds us. I have enjoyed our . . . er . . . conversation. This matter of great moment you have discovered—we shall talk of it another time."

He was gone, melting into the shadows so that Harriet could almost have believed she had never seen him. As upon another occasion, she had only the tenderness of her lips and the heavy beat of her heart to tell her that he had been there.

Assuring Sophy that she had merely slipped out for a breath of fresh air, she accompanied her back to the salon, where they found Lady Phoebe chatting to the Burbridges.

Released from his duties, Lord Burbridge was finding the time to entertain his wife's friends, and even Philip had forgotten his troubles long enough to listen eagerly to Lord Burbridge discussing certain matters appertaining to one of the latest Bills to go through Parliament.

Harriet could tell from Lord Burbridge's keen glance that he was impressed by Philip's grasp of political intricacies. Perhaps Lord Burbridge might do something to aid Philip's career, she thought hopefully. Perhaps work would take his mind off Lady Mary.

Even as she formed the thought, Harriet saw Philip's eyes straying toward the red-haired woman. She was wearing a gown of crimson silk—like darting tongues of flame, Harriet thought distastefully, as though the lovely white body were being devoured by fire. Telling herself she was growing too fanciful, Harriet looked away.

"Well, Miss Willoughby, still planning my downfall?"

Even though she knew no one else could have overheard the mocking words, Harriet glanced fearfully at her aunt.

"She has not heard me," the Comte drawled, reading her mind with ease. "She is too busy listening to Lady Burbridge. Well, are you not going to answer my question?"

"And what question is that, Charles, or can I quess?" asked Lord Burbridge, making Harriet jump as he smiled genially down at her. "Were you soliciting Miss Willoughby's hand for a waltz? I wish I were twenty years younger myself. In my day we never got closer to our partners than an arm's length."

"I doubt if anyone could persuade Miss Willoughby to dance with me," the Comte murmured drily. "She would consider it very unpatriotic indeed, wouldn't you, my child?"

Harriet cast him an indignant look, while Lord Burbridge, plainly amused, looked first at the Comte and then at Harriet before asking, "Oh? And why should she do that?"

"Because, my dear Burbridge, she thinks me a French spy," announced the Comte coolly, his eyes alight with mockery.

"A French spy, you?" Lord Burbridge laughed heartily, wiping his eyes with an immaculate handkerchief. When he had sobered up a little, he took one of Harriet's small hands between his own. "Forgive me, child, but *Charles*—a *spy*—and I suppose the rogue has teased you unmercifully for it!"

Harriet wished the ground would open up and swallow her. He had done this deliberately, she thought fiercely, giving the Comte a look that should have instantly transformed him to stone. Unfortunately he appeared to be engrossed in studying the dancers, through an elegant eyeglass he was holding with every appearance of bored disdain.

"Miss Willoughby would appear to have a powerful imagination," he drawled at length.

"Come, Charles, you are being too hard on her," Lord Burbridge said comfortingly. "A mistake, eh, Miss Willoughby?"

A mistake indeed, thought Harriet gritting her teeth, but it was not hers. Oh, he had tricked her nicely, making her look a complete fool. It was on the tip of her tongue to denounce him here and now—to tell Lord Burbridge about the smuggler and the occasion when she had found the Comte rifling his desk, but good sense prevailed. Let the Comte have his moment of triumph. Soon it would be her turn, and the tables would be turned with a vengeance!

"So, we are all agreed, it was nothing more than a mistake," reiterated Lord Burbridge in a kindly fashion. "Charles, I suggest you ask Miss Willoughby for this next waltz. And you, Miss Willoughby," he said, turning to Harriet, "must accept him. The waltz will be your peace-treaty, eh?"

There was little Harriet could say. Plainly there was nothing to be gained in stating again that the Comte was a spy. She would just have to find another way of convincing Lord Burbridge. In this instance the Comte had been far too clever for her, but if she could find some concrete evidence of his guilt . . .

Harriet sighed as the Comte led her onto the floor. They danced in silence until the Comte murmured softly, "You will have to sharpen your weapons if you wish to do battle with me, you know."

Harriet did not deign to reply. Out of the corner of her eye she saw Lady Mary advance upon them, her green eyes glittering with malice. She placed long, white fingers on the Comte's arm, drawling huskily, "There you are, Charles. I have been looking for you this age. I want to leave. It is so boring here." Her eyes dropped to Harriet. "Philip is coming with me. I thought perhaps we would go to Susan Harding's gaming. I feel lucky tonight, and Philip has promised to stake me."

Harriet thought her gasp of dismay had escaped unnoticed, but when Lady Mary turned away, the Comte said sardonically, "You cannot protect him forever, you know. Sometime he must learn what the world is."

"But must he learn it such a hard way?" Harriet stormed rebelliously. "Do you *want* him to be destroyed, is that it?"

chapter eight

The clubroom of White's was fairly crowded when the Comte strolled in at a little after eleven o'clock. One or two acquaintances called out greetings, one young would-be dandy eyeing him affably and drawling, "Lord save us, Comte, this is a new come-out, ain't it? The other morning your man told me you never stirred outside until after midday!"

"He must be confusing me with his previous master," the Comte replied lazily. "I understand he once valeted Beau Brummell."

"Very neat, la Valle," murmured a gentleman engaged in a hand of whist, "but I shouldn't mention Brummell in here if I was you. He's out of favor with Prinny these days, and badly dipped, too, by all accounts. Do you fancy a hand?" he asked, gesturing toward the table.

The Comte shook his head. "Not this morning, Stainton. Another time perhaps."

"Umm," mused the card-player when the Comte was out of earshot. "I wonder what brings him here so early?"

"Perhaps he's looking for young Wyclyffe," suggested one of his companions. "The boy's all out to make a fool of himself, over Lady Mary."

"Aye, so I've heard. Young idiot! Does de la Valle mean to let him get away with it, d'you suppose?"

Since none of the card-players could give an acceptable answer to this conundrum, they were obliged to abandon the fascinating subject of the Comte and return to their game.

The Comte paused by the portals of the Members' Room, murmuring a few words of enquiry to a hovering flunkey before, apparently satisfied with his response, he sauntered over to a young gentleman deep in the pages of the *Morning Post*.

Edward Danvers was engrossed in a report on the war in the Peninsula when the Comte's shadow fell across the table. Startled, he glanced upward, returning the Comte's "Good morning" while wondering why a gentleman so far outside his normal circle of acquaintances should have sought him out.

"You are studying the reports from the Peninsula, I see," the Comte drawled when they had both been served with wine. "They make good reading—for the English and those of us French who hope to see the monarchy restored."

Privately, Edward doubted if the French would ever accept the insipid Bourbon monarch as their King, but being a polite young gentleman, refrained from saying as much to his companion.

"They say Wellington is an inspired commander," commented the Comte. "It is your own wish to serve under him, perhaps?"

Startled that the Comte should have read his mind with such ease, Edward allowed that this was so. It was his greatest hope that his regiment might be posted to the Peninsula. Once there he had every hope that he would soon gain advancement and thus be in a better position to offer for Sophy.

"I should like to," Edward admitted. "I have my own way to make in the world and . . ."

"Miss Wyclyffe's mama is something of a stumbling block?" suggested the Comte, smiling a little.

"I'm afraid Lady Phoebe does not look kindly on my suit," Edward agreed ruefully, "but I cannot blame her. Sophy is the loveliest of creatures and deserving of far better than a mere Captain who will never earn more than a beggarly pittance!"

"So, love's path does not run smoothly?" asked the Comte easily. "And yet you seem to contrive. I am sure I have seen you in Hatchards with Miss Wyclyffe and her cousin."

"Yes, Harriet has helped us snatch what meetings we can," Edward admitted. "She is very fond of her cousins."

"But perhaps fonder of Master Philip Wyclyffe?" suggested the Comte softly.

Edward owned to a small feeling of unease. Quite how the conversation had moved from Wellington's armies in the Peninsular War and his own future to a discussion of Harriet Willoughby's fondness for her cousin Philip he was not too sure, but he did recognize a master tactician when he saw one!

"As to that, I could not say," he replied rather stiffly, feeling a little foolish when he saw the amusement gleaming in the Comte's eyes.

"Of course," drawled the Frenchman smoothly, "it is a bad *ton* for us to discuss the lady in such a fashion, I agree. Let us talk of something else then."

Edward was just congratulating himself on dealing with the situation very adroitly indeed when the Comte turned the tables and drawled, "Young Wyclyffe himself, for instance. Am I right in thinking the boy has barely a feather to fly with?"

Wondering uncomfortably what malign fate had caused him to be sitting in the Members' Room at the precise moment of the Comte's entry, Edward shrugged uneasily. "As to that, certainly he is not wealthy," he agreed, "but Sir George is possessed of a handsome estate and—"

"Umm," murmured the Comte, interrupting, "but however fond a parent Sir George is, I doubt he would look favorably upon his son's present mode of conduct."

It was too pointed to be ignored. "I collect you are referring to the Lady Mary, Comte," he said quietly. "That is a matter for yourself and Wyclyffe. If you must have it, I own it is not a connection his family can like, and they would doubtless be grateful for any intervention on your part."

"But they would *not* thank me for pushing the young fool into a position from which he could not escape with honor," suggested the Comte drily.

Edward succumbed to the helpless sensation that somehow matters had passed completely from his control.

"If you mean to challenge Wyclyffe to a duel," he began hesitantly, only to be silenced by the Comte's curt, *"Dieu! A duel! Over a woman of the demi-mondaine!"*

Sensitive to the scorn in the other's voice, Edward felt a twinge of pity for the woman they were discussing.

"Then if you do not intend to challenge Wyclyffe," he asked helplessly, "what is the purpose of our conversation?"

"The purpose," the Comte drawled laconically, "has already been accomplished. The rest was but a re-affirmation of what I already suspected." He smiled quizzically into Edward's indignant face. "Don't worry, Danvers, I do not intend to challenge Wyclyffe. If he is so enamoured of Lady Mary, then let him have her!"

Leaving Edward to wrestle with his bewilderment, the Comte sauntered out of White's in much the same fashion as he had entered it. Despite the Comte's urbane charm, Edward was convinced he was playing some deep game, and as he drained his glass and turned his attention back to the *Post*, he shook his head and murmured under his breath, "Poor Philip!"

Poor Philip indeed! While the Comte and Edward had been conversing over a glass of claret, he was walking disconsolately in the direction of his rooms in Half Moon Street, still unable to comprehend the enormity of the coil in which he found himself.

Arriving home in the early hours of the morning, he had wakened with an aching head and a dim recollection of a small pile of vouchers mounting before him on a green baize table. He had spent the morning in a musty little room off Cranbourne Alley—the haunt of money-lenders and pawnbrokers—where he had parted with his fob and a ring that had once belonged to the Wyclyffe who sailed with Drake. Even now he doubted that he had sufficient to meet his debts, and even while he cursed himself for a fool, the recollection of Lady Mary sent his blood pounding through his veins, so that all else paled into insignificance in comparison to his longing for her.

Halfway back to his lodgings, Philip changed his mind and redirected his footsteps toward South Audley Street. At least there he would find companionship and, he hoped, an escape from his own unpleasant thoughts. A man in love made a poor companion, he reflected mirthlessly, for himself and everyone else.

Philip found Harriet and Sophy in the blue sitting room, seated before the fire, roasting chestnuts and perusing magazines. Soothed by the normality of the cosy scene, Philip drew up a chair and relieved Harriet of her toasting fork.

"Goodness, Philip, you are quite the

stranger," Sophy commented waspishly. "Has Lady Mary given you the go-by, then?"

Philip frowned and would have retorted had the maid not come in with a message for Sophy to go to the sewing room, where Mrs. Fitch was waiting to fit her new gown.

Alone with her cousin, Harriet's heart ached for the shadows in Philip's eyes and the new hardness about his face.

"Can't you tell me what troubles you, Philip?" she asked softly, prompted by a recollection of their younger days, when Philip himself had often encouraged her to confide in him her childish troubles.

A bitter smile twisted Philip's mouth. "And damn myself forever in your eyes, Harriet?" He squeezed her hand gently. "Thank you, coz, but I will not burden you with this. My problems are all of my own making."

"Papa says that to share a problem is sometimes to solve it," Harriet offered persuasively, adding gently, "You need not fear to shock me, Philip. I have learned a good deal more of the world since I came to London, and I already have an inkling of what taxes you. It's Lady Mary, isn't it?"

Philip laughed harshly. "Dear God, Harriet, I am not one of your father's worthy parishioners. Your mama's slave cannot soothe my wound. I should be thrice cursed for even allowing you to guess at what is on my mind. It is not fitting . . ." He broke off, his voice suddenly suspended. What had happened to him that he even considering discussing his cares with his innocent cousin? Dear Harriet, what could she know of the devils that drove him, she who only saw good in the worst of persons and thought everyone lived by her own strict codes?

Looking into Philip's drawn face, Harriet felt another surge of anger against the Comte. Surely he could have prevented Lady Mary from drawing Philip into the web of her beauty if he had so wished? Rather repressively, Harriet told herself that she had yet again been caught unawares by the unprincipled fashion in which the Comte continually seemed to take possession of her waking hours. It was strange how she was constantly envisaging his arrogantly mocking face, or recalling his cool, sardonic voice. Allowing him to dominate so many of her thoughts was a dangerous practice, as Harriet was the first to admit, but on this occasion surely there was every excuse for her thoughts to wing their way to the person of the Comte. After all, was he not indirectly responsible for Philip's present predicament?

Philip was staring morosely into the fire, the chestnuts forgotten. Harriet touched his hand commiseratingly. "What is it, Philip? Did you lose a great deal last night?"

Philip gave a start and stared at her with haunted eyes. "How did you know?"

Harriet thought it pointless to remind him that she had witnessed his exit from Carlton House with Lady Mary. Instead she smiled sympathetically and begged him to confide in his father.

"Sir George is not a strict father, Philip," she reminded him. "He will understand how it is." With a wisdom that sat oddly on her slender shoulders, Harriet added hesitantly, "Of course, I do not know a great deal of these matters, but Papa has often told me that gambling has destroyed more men than war."

Philip smiled a little at that, although not very cheerfully. He could just about cover his debts on this occasion, and although Harriet was correct when she said Sir George was a fond parent, Philip felt that his pride would not permit him to go to his father and admit what a fool he had been. And yet, he admitted helplessly, if Lady Mary were to come to him again, he could not say that he would be able to resist her siren call.

He shuddered a little, burying his head in his hands. At his side Harriet watched him compassionately. There was no room in her now for any jealousy of Lady Mary. Without her being aware of it, her adoring worship of Philip had changed from a young girl's first tender infatuation to the wiser, more understanding love of a sister.

"You will forget her in time, Philip. One day you will love—"

"Love!" Philip burst out with a groan. "God, Harriet, you can't even begin to know what you are talking about. You, who have no knowledge of love other than the tepid emotion you have learned of in your father's library."

"Philip, I . . ."

"Don't tell me you understand," he said ruthlessly, "for you cannot. How could you even begin to comprehend the madness that eats into a man's soul—you to whom a man's kisses are still the chaste embraces of a brother!"

His bitterness was not directed toward her, Harriet knew that, nor did Philip guess how very far from the truth his accusations were, but she felt a shaft of pain, that he should think her still no more than a young child, to be protected from the realities of life.

Philip was facing the window, lost in his own unhappy thoughts. Outside a carriage drove past; two ladies were taking the morning air, their maids in discreet attendance—a blessedly normal scene, but it did nothing to alleviate his own private hell.

"I'm sorry, Harriet," he said jerkily, "I should not have spoken so."

He would have said more, but Lady Phoebe entered the room, plainly surprised to find her son there. She greeted him affectionately, frowning a little over his haggard countenance.

"You are doing too much, Philip," she scolded, "Lady Burbridge is calling this afternoon; why don't you join us? She was only remarking the other day that they are short-staffed at the Foreign Office; perhaps Lord Burbridge would put in a good word for you."

Philip smiled wanly, assuring his mother that he was both eating and sleeping properly (a lie!). The Foreign Office held no appeal for him, he told her lightly; Parliament was his goal, and not even Lady Phoebe's protestations that the Foreign Office would be a step in the right direction had the power to move him.

When he eventually took his leave of them Lady Phoebe looked decidedly uneasy. She sent Harriet upstairs to remind Sophy that Lady Burbridge was expected, asking with surprising hesitancy, when Harriet was at the door, if she felt that Philip was perhaps laboring under some dark cloud.

Harriet did not know what to say. She knew her aunt must be aware of the gossip about Lady Mary, but she was reluctant to add to her unhappiness by confiding in her her own fears for Philip.

Besides, Harriet reminded herself on her way upstairs, her conversation with Philip had been in the nature of a confidence! Rather grimly she admitted that for Philip and herself it might have been better had they never set eyes upon either the Comte or his mistress. Such a line of reasoning was not conducive to good spirits, Harriet chided herself; indeed; rather the opposite, for it reminded her of matters she would far rather forget!

It was plain from the moment Lady Burbridge entered the drawing room that she was greatly perturbed. She accepted a cup of tea from Lady Phoebe, sipping it absently, her normally clear brow furrowed with anxiety. What ailed her, Harriet wondered?

She was soon to know. Refusing a second cup of tea, Lady Burbridge leaned forward in her chair, her eyes fixed on Lady Phoebe's face.

"You will never guess, Phoebe! The most dreadful occurrence! I promise you I am quite distraught! For such a thing to happen!" A much-crumpled lawn handkerchief bore evidence of the state of her emotions as she twisted it nervously in her hands. "Some highly secret papers have gone missing from Burbridge's desk! I cannot conceive how it happened! It has given me the most wretched megrim, for the servants have the *strictest* orders never to go in Burbridge's study without permission, you must know. Only Burbridge himself and Mr. Fiennes are allowed to touch the desk!"

Lady Burbridge broke off and dabbed ineffectually at her eyes with the remnants of her shredded handkerchief.

"Burbridge has not blamed *me*—such a gentleman—but I cannot help feeling quite wretchedly low. To think that through my carelessness that dreadful Boney might. . ."

Here her voice was suspended completely. Harriet and Lady Phoebe made haste to reassure her that the blame was not hers, Harriet all the while tormented by the memory of the Comte bent over Lord Burbridge's open desk drawer. Why, oh, why had she not spoken! Unbidden the recollection of the Comte's amusement rose before her! What a fool he had made of her! Something at which the Comte was unusually adept, Harriet thought, remembering the assured fashion in which he had announced her suspicions to Lord Burbridge. Why, oh, why had she not stood her ground then, and denounced him? It was a question she could not answer. She came out of her daze to hear Lady Burbridge saying wretchedly, "Oh, yes, it is all quite dreadful. One of the papers was a list of all the British agents in France, and poor Burbridge cannot get it out of his mind that once it falls into French hands —as we can only suppose it must—their lives will all be forfeit."

The ladies fell silent. At last Harriet asked

timidly, "Could the list have been purloined by a member of the Bourbon entourage, perhaps?"

While Lady Phoebe frowned at her niece, Lady Burbridge shook her head decisively. "Oh, no. All the members of King Louis's party were rigorously investigated before they entered the country. The Comte is most concerned about it all. He has gone to the Foreign Office with Burbridge to see if he can throw any light upon the affair."

The man had the nerve of the devil, Harriet thought mirthlessly. His concern, if indeed he ever experienced such an emotion, must all be channelled toward ensuring that the all-important list reached the hands of England's enemies. It was intolerable, she reflected helplessly. How could she unmask him when the very people he was betraying persisted in regarding him as above suspicion?

"Oh, dear, now I have cast you all into gloom," Lady Burbridge exclaimed guiltily. "Sophy, when am I to congratulate you?" she asked archly. "Twice this week I have seen you in Hatchards with Edward. Such a very charming couple." Lady Burbridge appealed to Lady Phoebe, "I expect you will want Sophy to be presented before anything is announced?"

In the silence that followed, Lady Burbridge glanced helplessly from Sophy's guilty face to her mama's set one, and realizing that something was amiss, offered at last, "Oh, dear, I . . . ."

Not for the first time since her emergence from the schoolroom, Lady Phoebe was obliged to banish her daughter to her bedchamber, adding the rider that Harriet might as well accompany her cousin, for Lady Phoebe had something she wished to discuss with Lady Burbridge —in private!

In arctic accents Lady Phoebe informed her guest that Sophy, with only the smallest portion to come to her from her father, was expected to marry well! Lady Burbridge sympathized. Of course, she had not properly understood the matter, but, she promised her hostess, she would be sure to drop a word to the wise in Edward's ear. "It is the greatest shame that he has nothing to come to him from his grandfather's estate."

Icily Lady Phoebe concurred, although it would take a good deal more than a paltry allowance from the Marquis to make her view Captain Danvers with anything even approaching composure.

The household at South Audley Street sat down to dinner in an oppressive silence. Philip's health had faded into insignificance in the light of Sophy's shockingly improper behavior and throughout the meal Lady Phoebe refused to address so much as a single word to her erring and unrepentant daughter, save to tell her that she had already sent a note round to the Marquis laying the whole before him and advising him to deal as firmly by his grandson as she intended to do by her daughter.

"Oh, no, aunt. Surely you could not be so cruel!" Harriet protested, horrified by her aunt's grim statement.

"What's that, miss?" asked Lady Phoebe sharply. "Do you dare to question me?"

A helpless shake of Sophy's head warned

Harriet that she was protesting in vain. Subsiding into her chair, she applied herself to her dinner, although without much appetite. All that had transpired since her arrival in London was directly attributable to the enigmatic person of the Comte de la Valle, she thought wrathfully.

Harriet was still struggling to find a satisfactory method of bringing him to book when she retired for the night. A faint scratching at her door interrupted this course of thought, and Harriet opened it to admit Sophy, tear-stained and patently unhappy.

"Quickly, Harriet, before Mama discovers I am gone from my room! Promise me you will find a way to meet Edward at Hatchards tomorrow? Promise me?" she begged piteously.

Harriet promised. Lady Phoebe rarely rose before noon, and there should be plenty of time for Harriet to go to Hatchards and back before her aunt discovered she was missing. Perhaps the stimulation of a brisk walk might produce some means of proving to people that the Comte was a spy!

It occurred to Harriet as she dressed hurriedly in her pelisse and boots that so far the Comte had outwitted her at every turn. This state of affairs must not be allowed to continue, she thought firmly as she stepped outside.

Overnight the rain had gone and the sky was a soft, pale blue, the merest suggestion of a fluffy white cloud edging the distant horizon. The flagways gleamed after their cleansing of the previous day, and more than one person stopped to glance a second time at Harriet's neat figure in her lemon gown and matching pelisse. Unaware that she was the cynosure of so much interest, Harriet hurried on her way, deeply engrossed in her own thoughts.

Edward was waiting for her, patiently anxious.

"Sophy?" he asked the moment Harriet was seated. "Is she all right?"

Only when Harriet had been able to reassure him on this all-important point did Edward relax enough to tell her of his grandfather's reaction to Lady Phoebe's note.

"It could not have happened at a worse time," he told Harriet ruefully. "My grandfather received news yesterday that my cousin has been wounded. Roger is his heir, and naturally he is greatly concerned for him. He wanted him to sell out when his regiment was posted to the Peninsula, but Roger refused."

Harriet sympathized. It was only natural that the Marquis should be concerned for his grandson, and she could well imagine how infuriated he would have been on receiving Lady Phoebe's letter.

Edward had no intention of telling her that his grandfather, plagued by gout and anxious for the recovery of his heir, had told him in no uncertain terms that he was a fool if he wasted himself on a mere country chit with nothing but a pretty face to recommend her, adding unkindly that if Edward hoped that *he* was going to come up with the "ready," then he could think again!

He had paid for Edward's education, the Marquis reminded him, aye, and bought him his captaincy into the bargain, and that was as much as he was prepared to do.

It had been a short, if acrimonious, step from this to a recollection of how Edward's father had defied him, and it had only been with the greatest difficulty that the younger man had held onto his temper. It was pointless to regret Lady Burbridge's idle comment now, but then he supposed they had courted from the very first meeting in such a very public place.

Harriet was so sympathetic that Edward found himself pouring out all his hopes to her. How he had planned to impress Sir George with his swift rise through the ranks and his determination to ensure that Sophy should not suffer from being his wife, but now he doubted if Sir George would even allow him to enter the Hall!

Harriet could think of nothing to comfort him. Poor Captain Danvers! His grandfather, he told Harriet heavily, had demanded that he return to Folkstone forthwith and put Sophy from his mind forever. The first command he was honor bound to obey, but the second was an impossibility he could not, and would not, countenance, on pain of death itself.

Giving Harriet a letter for Sophy, he begged her to assure the other girl of his undying love, adding that he would find a way for them to be reunited if Sophy would just be patient!

With Lady Phoebe's threats very much to the forefront of her mind Harriet wondered whether Sophy would be allowed to return to the Marsh without first contracting what her mama considered a "suitable" alliance. Too kind-hearted to put these fears into words, she assured Edward that she would deliver his message, and it was not until he had taken his leave of her and walked out into the street that Edward remembered he had meant to comment upon his strange conversation with the Comte.

He hesitated on the flagway, about to turn back, when he saw the Comte swing down from an impressive curricle, flinging the reins to a groom, before walking into Hatchards. Even as he watched, he saw the Comte pause and stare around the room as though searching for someone, before striding purposefully in the direction of Miss Willoughby.

At another time Edward might have found this a very strange circumstance indeed, but his thoughts were fully occupied on his own problems, and he did little more than reflect that it was an odd coincidence that brought the Comte to Hatchards at the very same time as the young lady he had been discussing only the previous day.

Harriet was as surprised to see the Comte as Edward had been.

"Alone, Miss Willoughby?" murmured the Comte as he bowed to a be-turbaned dowager.

"I cannot conceive that that is any business of yours," Harriet responded in freezing accents. "Please let me pass."

"Tell me, have you succeeded yet in convincing anyone of my guilt?"

"You are pleased to mock me, sir," Harriet said. "I suppose you will now tell me that the circumstance of my finding you in Lord Burbridge's room at the same time as a secret document went missing is the merest figment of my imagination also?"

"Isn't it?" drawled the Comte quizzically, but Harriet thought she detected a sharpening of the gray eyes as they rested on her face. "You are treading dangerous ground, my dear. After all, who is to say that *you* did not purloin Lord Burbridge's papers?"

Harriet went white at the unexpectedness of the thrust.

"I?" she breathed indignantly. "Why should I want to do such a thing?"

"Why should you not?" countered the Comte. "There are those who would pay well for such information, and you are a young lady of no great fortune. Think how very much more attractive you would appear as a bride for young Wyclyffe with a handsome dowry behind you."

Harriet was too shocked by his suggestion to do more than stare, dumbfounded. When she at last found her breath, she stammered disbelievingly, "Do you actually dare to suggest that *I* would stoop so low as to . . . to . . ."

"Why not?" said the Comte carelessly. "After all, it is no worse than you have attributed to me. Do you suppose my sense of honor to be less keen than your own, Miss Willoughby?"

"I collect we have different understandings of the word 'honor' sir!" Harriet flashed back, "and now if you will let me pass."

She was not prepared for the savagery of his fingers as they bit into her arm. Above her, his eyes were glittering with an emotion she could not name, his face harsh and thin-lipped, so that she barely recognized the suave Comte in the person who now bent over her.

"One day you will try me too far," he warned her grimly. "I am a man, Miss Willoughby, made up of blood, flesh, and emotion like any other. I am not a stone statue to be insulted at will by an ignorant miss who thinks herself free to cast all manner of aspersions upon my character. Up until now I have been disposed to deal gently with you, but when you impugn my honor you go too far."

He released her and walked out of the bookshop, swinging himself up into his curricle with something less than his usual grace. The incident had been too brief to be observed by anyone, and yet Harriet was left with the devastating impression that those few seconds had somehow changed the course of her whole life, although she was at a loss to understand why.

The Comte was her enemy—a man who would destroy her country and yet for a moment, in his anger, had shown all the muted fury of a man who feels himself wronged. Just another of his ploys to disarm her, Harriet told herself fiercely. Well, this time he would not catch her off guard!

chapter nine

Lady Phoebe had still not forgiven Sophy by the end of the week. Her displeasure had also extended to include Harriet, who, she considered, had encouraged Sophy in her willful defiance.

Casting around for a suitable means of punishment, she at first had it in mind to forbid the acceptance of Lady Burbridge's generous invitation to a party she intended to make up for the Fireworks Display and Grand Ball to be held at Vauxhall Gardens as part of the Regency Celebrations.

Lady Burbridge, calling expressly to deliver this invitation, confided that normally she would not have countenanced a party at Vauxhall, for all the world knew that it had deteriorated sadly from the days when Horace Walpole went there by boat and Handel's music had been played in the pavilions. The days when satin-clad gentlemen flirted elegantly in the boxes belonged to the past, and nowadays one was more likely to encounter half a dozen young Tulips of Fashion in the Long Walk, ogling the Cyprians who plied their trade in what had once been the haunt of the *beau monde*.

However, Lady Burbridge assured Lady Phoebe that on *this* occasion there could be nothing to cavil at in their attending. All the world and his wife would be going, and it promised to be a very splendid affair indeed and a far cry from the formality of the Carlton House dinner.

When Lady Phoebe pursed her lips, neither Sophy nor Harriet had been able to breathe for fear lest she vetoed the suggestion, but when she collected that denying the girls the treat would necessarily mean denying herself, and a further moment's pause reminded her of the existence of a very fine new turban, dashingly trimmed with the ostrich feathers they had purchased, and as yet still unworn, she decided to relent.

Happily, for the peace of mind of at least two members of her party, Lady Burbridge did not have time to expound upon the nature of her other guests, and the night of the ball dawning fine and clear, the South Audley Street household found themselves with little else to do but dress themselves in their best gowns and await the carriage to transport them to the pleasure gardens.

Sophy had elected to wear her favorite pale

blue, this time a demure gown with pearl-embroidered sleeves and hem. The pearls, she confided unhappily to Harriet, could denote the tears she had cried for Edward.

The week had brought no further news of him, and forbidden to so much as mention his name, Sophy had no idea of whether he was still in London or whether he had actually returned to the Marsh. Harriet comforted her as best she could, standing away from the cheval glass to appraise her appearance in her peach ninon. Delicate silver vine leaves curled upward from the hem, the motif repeated on the bodice. The dainty diamond necklace that had been Papa's wedding gift to her mama circled her slender neck, and although she was no beauty, Harriet reflected modestly, she would not discredit her aunt.

Obediently sitting down so that the maid could thread silver ribbons through her curls, she advised Sophy to have patience, reminding her of Edward's promise to get in touch. Sophy refused to be reassured. Edward had quite forgotten her, she exclaimed tearfully, and she could not think *why* she was going to this dreary ball when he would not be there, and her mama would doubtless expect her to dance with all manner of suitable young men!

"You don't know how lucky you are that *your* mama married for love," Sophy exclaimed. "She would never force *you* to an unwanted marriage."

While acknowledging the truth of this statement, Harriet was obliged to admit that her mother would be pleased and relieved if she were to contract an advantageous marriage as a result of her stay in London. Without saying so in as many words, Elizabeth Willoughby had communicated to Harriet her hopes of this season in London.

Harriet bit her lip. There had been any number of charming gentlemen who had begged to be introduced to her, some of whom, she knew without vanity, would have liked to further the acquaintance. Somehow or other, none of them had touched any answering chord within her, and although she admitted that at first she had been blinded by her infatuation for Philip, now she had no excuse to look askance at the hopeful recipients of her favors.

Indeed, she realized, with a perplexed frown, she had spent so much time worrying about the nefarious behavior of the Comte de la Valle that there had been none left for dalliance.

There had been several very eligible young men introduced to her by Lady Burbridge, but when she tried to recall their faces, they remained a maddening blur, superseded by the Comte's arrogant countenance.

"Harriet, you are dreaming!" Sophy accused, handing her a Norwich silk shawl with silver embroidery, which had been lying on the bed. "Mama says you are to hurry. The carriage is at the door." Flushing a little guiltily, Harriet did as she was bidden.

Philip, whose continued absence from South Audley Street had caused his mother no little concern, arrived just in time to hand the ladies into the carriage. He, too, presented a very elegant appearance, although Harriet's fond eye denoted an increasing pallor in the familiar features. As he closed the carriage door, he managed to give Harriet's fingers a comforting squeeze, but he was so quiet and subdued on the way to the Gardens that she was drawn to the reluctant conclusion that his involvement with Lady Mary was as intense as ever.

Lady Burbridge was waiting for them in the main pavilion. Lord Burbridge was with her, and another gentleman, somberly attired, who was introduced as Edward's grandfather. However, it was not his presence, strange as it seemed in the gaily clad throng of revellers, that drew a dismayed gasp from Harriet as the introductions were performed, but the sardonic smile the Comte bestowed upon her when Harriet realized that he, too, was included in Lady Burbridge's party!

Her initial dismay was increased when the Comte raised her fingers to his lips. An old-fashioned gesture, but quite pointed, Harriet felt, withdrawing her hand as though she had been stung.

"Charles, you are embarrassing Miss Willoughby," Lord Burbridge chided indulgently, adding to Harriet, "Take no notice of him, my dear, he is a wicked tease at times."

Tease or not, Harriet thought darkly, from now on she would watch the Comte like the proverbial hawk. Sooner or later, he must surely betray himself!

Harriet was not the only one to be dismayed by Lady Burbridge's choice of guests. Lady Phoebe was none too pleased to discover that Captain Danvers was included in the party, and a very stern look in her daughter's direction warned her of her mama's views on the subject.

Sophy refused to heed it. With shining eyes she whispered to Harriet that nothing would spoil her pleasure in what threatened to be her last moments with Edward.

Lady Burbridge intercepted Lady Phoebe's warning glance and leaned across to murmur apologetically, "Edward insisted, and I did not have the heart to refuse him!"

In fact Edward's appearance was not to be the only surprise the evening held in store.

They watched the fireworks from grandstand seats procured by Lord Burbridge, both young girls breathless with awe as the glittering tableaux exploded in a dazzling array of brilliantly colored stars. Watching a crimson sunburst fall to earth, Harriet was moved to murmur, "How marvelous! How do they do that, do you suppose?"

"They use a form of gunpowder," the Comte informed her drily, making her start, for she had not seen him standing behind her. "Do you know, for a moment then, Miss Willoughby, you reminded me of a child."

Harriet flushed. For some unknown reason, her heart was beating uncomfortably fast. "You are pleased to make fun of me, sir," she said stiffly. "No doubt you find my lack of worldliness amusing."

Her eyes flashed dangerously, but the Comte ignored them, his expression unreadable as Harriet stared up toward him. The others had moved slightly away, and for a moment Harriet felt they could have been alone in the entire universe.

"Amusing? I think not," replied the Comte unexpectedly. "Salutary, rather."

Harriet would have pressed him to explain, but they were interrupted by Lady Phoebe exclaiming direfully that Sophy had disappeared. While the other members of the party glanced about them, the culprit returned on Edward Danvers's arm, her face alight with joy.

"Sophy!" Lady Phoebe began chidingly.

"No, Mama, don't say anything yet," Sophy begged, turning a radiant face up to Edward. "May I tell her now?" she asked him breathlessly. Not waiting for a reply, she burst out, "Mama, you will never guess. Edward's cousin has died!" She lowered her voice, glancing toward the Marquis, who was deep in conversation with Lord Burbridge.

"Edward is now the Marquis's direct heir. He will inherit everything," she said simply, to her astounded mama. "Of course, it will mean we can only have the very smallest wedding, and Edward will have to go into black, but the Marquis has agreed that he will help Edward buy himself out of the army, and once we are married we are to live at Upton—that is his principal seat you must know. And . . ."

"Naturally, I shall pay my addresses to Sir George," Edward interposed swiftly. "But I cannot help feeling that in view of my changed circumstances . . . In fact, my grandfather was only persuaded to come here tonight especially to see Sophy." Edward pulled a rueful face. "He did not want me to make the same mistake he considered my father made, but I think I have convinced him of the depth of my regard."

"Edward told him he would refuse the title if the Marquis did not give his consent," Sophy explained with an adoring look at her discomfited suitor. "You cannot refuse to let us marry now, Mama."

Lady Phoebe was lost for words. Two thoughts struggled simultaneously for expression; the first being her amazement at Edward's sudden change of fortune and the second her chagrin that the Marquis should dare to doubt the worthiness of *her* daughter to be the next Marchioness.

Fortunately, discretion won the day. She bestowed a very cool smile upon Edward, congratulating him on his good fortune, and answered Sophy's importunings with the information that she would write to Sir George straightway to appraise him of Captain Danvers's intentions.

When the Marquis finally ceased his discussion with Lord Burbridge and told her gruffly that Sophy was a "taking little thing," she allowed graciously that the child was perhaps a little flighty, but that no doubt marriage would mend matters, especially with the young couple so very much in love.

Rather tentatively she offered her condolences on the death of his eldest grandson, wishing the circumstances did not make her feel that such sentiments could hardly sound genuine, but the Marquis smiled briefly, the action suddenly making him look very much like his young relative.

"I was fond of the boy, and that I'll not deny, but young Edward will make a good landlord. He's a stayer, and that's what this country needs nowadays. No need to put the wedding off. The sooner Upton's nurseries are filled, the better, eh, my Lady?"

Rather taken aback by this frank statement, Lady Phoebe murmured an appropriate comment and expressed herself relieved that the Marquis was taking his loss so sensibly.

No one was really surprised when, after pinching Sophy's flushed cheek and congratulating his grandson, the Marquis took his leave.

"It is the greatest shame that Edward's inheritance comes to him in such a tragic fashion," Lady Burbridge said later. "But for all that the Marquis was so fond of him, Roger had a wild streak. Of the two, Edward will make the best successor to his title. Of course, there can be no question of him not being a suitable *parti* for Sophy now," she added to Lady Phoebe. "Indeed I expect there will be those who will think Sophy has done very well for herself!"

Lady Phoebe acknowledged this thrust. She had been speedily reviewing the subject and had come to the unpalatable conclusion that Lady Burbridge was quite right. As the direct heir of the Marquis, Edward could have chosen from amongst the highest in the land. The young people's desire for an early marriage must certainly be encouraged, Lady Phoebe decided. It was the greatest pity that mourning prevented her from indulging in the flurry of extravagant preparations she would have wished, but there could be nothing to cavil at in her giving a very small party at the Hall to celebrate the betrothal. Already she was planning exactly how she would break the news to the Duchess. (That good lady had dared to allow just the merest hint of condescension to creep into her voice when reviewing Sophy's possible success in London.) Lady Phoebe heaved a satisfied sigh.

Edward, from being merely "Captain Danvers and of no account" was suddenly her "dearest boy"—a transformation that brought a twinkle to Harriet's eyes as she listened to her aunt's rhapsodies.

In the babble of excited congratulations Harriet saw the Comte detach himself from the small group and disappear into the darkness.

Her hands curled into small fists. Where was he going? A rendezvous with Lady Mary? Harriet doubted it. He had left with a more purposeful tread than that engendered by a mere romantic interlude.

Stirred by indecision, she stared after him. Could this be her opportunity to discover some concrete evidence of his treachery? Silently she slid after him. With all the excitement, she doubted if anyone would notice she was missing, and it was too good an opportunity to waste.

At first it was easy to keep track of the Comte, for his broad shoulders were clearly discernible among the crowd, and Harriet found that by keeping a discreet half-dozen paces behind him, she was able to follow his progress quite easily. Thanking providence that she herself, being so small, was able to hide in the crowd, Harriet watched the Comte approach one of the many walks.

He hovered for a moment by the entrance, glancing over his shoulder so that Harriet was obliged to bend down and fiddle with her sandal so that she would not be observed.

When she raised her head, he was striding down the candlelit walk, the swaying lights casting long shadows among the trees.

Her heart in her mouth, Harriet slid after him, keeping well into the shadows, and hoping that she would not betray her presence.

The walk was empty save for the Comte and herself. He paused at length in a quieter part of the garden, where the sounds of revelry were no more than a muted ripple across the silence.

The fireworks display had finished, and people were drifting across to the main pavilion to listen to the musicians and watch the dancers.

The Comte glanced over his shoulder occasionally, each time making Harriet's heart give a suffocated bound. At every step she expected to be discovered. The path twisted and revealed a cunningly hidden pagoda, but the Comte barely glanced at it. Instead he sat down on one of the rustic benches dotted about the walk.

Harriet froze. She must find somewhere to hide, but where? A flowering cherry tree afforded some cover, and gratefully Harriet crouched against its sheltering trunk.

She did not have long to wait. She had barely composed herself when a man approached the Comte from the opposite end of the walk. When the Comte rose and greeted the newcomer, Harriet strained her ears, trying to overhear their conversation. It was no use! She was too far away. Well, she had not come this far to be cheated of victory now!

Slowly Harriet dodged forward, her tongue between her teeth as she tried to keep within the shadows of the tree. The ground was uneven, and she could feel the damp seeping into her thin slippers. A ballgown was not the best of things to wear for such work, Harriet admitted ruefully, as the ninon caught on a low branch and had to be carefully untangled.

She could hear snatches of conversation now. The gentlemen appeared to be arguing; at least one of them did; the Comte, true to form, appeared to be completely at ease, listening to his companion and occasionally interpolating a questioning remark.

It was so frustrating! If only she could get a little closer. She was sure it was no ordinary business that brought the Comte to this quiet part of the gardens, no mere matter of a chance-met acquaintance.

Both gentlemen were conversing in low voices.

"You will have to be patient!" she heard the Comte drawl.

His companion's response was muted, but Harriet could tell he was annoyed. He paced up and down and gestured wildly with his arms. Plainly he was not very pleased with whatever the Comte had told him.

"The matter grows urgent," Harriet heard him say to the Comte. "They are waiting . . ."

The rest was lost as a twig snapped under her foot. Stifling a gasp, Harriet crouched down.

In her anxiety not to miss anything, Harriet had grown careless. She froze as she heard the Comte's companion exclaim sharply, "What was that? Someone is there!"

"A bird or an animal," the Comte said soothingly with a shrug. "It was nothing."

Harriet breathed a sigh of relief. If they had come to investigate! She closed her eyes, shuddering as she pictured the Comte's face if he were to find her here.

She moved uncomfortably, her limbs grown stiff with cramp. A stone rolled out from beneath her, and with a protesting cry Harriet felt herself falling forward.

"Someone *is* there!"

There was a sudden movement, the firm tread of male feet invading her hiding place, and harsh fingers gripping her arm, and dragging her unceremoniously onto the lighted path.

"Well, well," drawled the Comte mercilessly. "Miss Willoughby!"

Harriet felt ready to die of mortification. The Comte was regarding her with a singular lack of surprise, but what the Comte failed to express, his companion more than made up for, peering into Harriet's face and exclaiming angrily, "*Mon dieu!* What is this? Were you spying on us, miss?"

His accent betrayed him as French, and while Harriet sought despairingly for some reasonable explanation for her presence, she was conscious of the Comte eyeing her with grim speculation.

"I was . . . waiting for someone," Harriet

invented wildly. "I must have mistaken the path I—"

"You certainly mistook *something!*" agreed the Comte drily. He glanced rather disdainfully at Harriet's untidy appearance. Her ringlets were in considerable disorder, she was sure, and her ankle was throbbing uncomfortably where she had fallen on it.

"You may safely leave Miss Willoughby in my hands, Jules," the Comte assured his companion. "Our business is concluded, I believe. I shall have the . . . er . . . package for you soon."

When the Frenchman had gone, he turned to survey Harriet. Those gray eyes missed nothing, Harriet thought uncomfortably, trying to smooth her crumpled gown, at the same time wondering if there was mud on her nose or leaves in her hair from her sojourn under the tree.

"A strange place to conduct your business, Comte," she said with an attempt at bravado she did not feel. She had once read somewhere that attack is the best method of defense. Obviously, the Comte had not read it, for he was continuing to regard her in a singularly unpleasant fashion.

"Hardly, when you yourself chose it as a meeting place. Although that *is* a circumstance I find 'strange,'" the Comte drawled. "That you should by some odd chance choose the same spot for your meeting as I did for my business. Who were you waiting for, by the way?" he asked blandly. "Or need I guess—young Wyclyffe, perchance?"

Harriet gulped with relief. "Yes . . . that is . . . I was meeting Philip," she said boldly, trying to avoid the Comte's raised eyebrow.

"Were you so?"

(Was it her imagination, or had his lazy drawl actually increased?)

"Strange, then, that *he* should be escorting Lady Mary. Or perhaps he has forgot his appointment?"

"Yes . . . yes, I suppose that must be the case," Harriet agreed frantically. Oh, how neatly he had trapped her. With what diabolical intent had he suggested she might have been meeting Philip. She might have known he only meant to trick her.

"It was not precisely an appointment," Harriet said loftily, recovering her slip. "It was just that we were to meet if neither of us was doing anything else."

The Comte raised a disbelieving eyebrow.

"Oh, come, Miss Willoughby. Credit me with some intelligence. There was no appointment. You were following me. I saw you when I turned into the walk."

Harriet gave a gasp of indignation.

"You mean you deliberately let me hide under that wretchedly uncomfortable tree and all the time . . ."

"All the time . . ." agreed the Comte with suspicious gravity. "However, the game ends here, my child. You have made your last throw and lost, are we agreed on that, at least?"

"Do you admit, then, that I *was* right and you are a spy?" Harriet asked in a small voice.

The Comte regarded her with a curious smile. "And if I did—what would you do?"

"Tell the authorities," Harriet said without hesitation. "Bring you to the justice you so richly deserve."

Vehement though her assertion was, it failed to bring her the sense of righteousness she had expected to feel. Instead, she was conscious of an empty feeling in the pit of her stomach.

"Such a very proper sentiment," mocked the Comte. "Perhaps it is fortunate, then, that I am going to tell you no such thing."

"But I saw you . . . I heard you—" Harriet —began heatedly, but the Comte interrupted her.

"You will forget all you have seen and heard, Miss Willoughby," he told her evenly.

"Forget? And if I say I shall not?" asked Harriet, her eyes kindling afresh at this calm assertion.

"Then in that case I should be obliged to use other methods of ensuring your silence," the Comte said firmly. "I am right in saying that you are particularly fond of young Wyclyffe, aren't I?" When Harriet stubbornly refused to reply he drawled, "Well, no matter, but let me warn you now, should you ever breathe one word of what has gone forward tonight, your cousin will live to rue the day."

"I am not frightened by your threats," Harriet said scornfully. "You cannot hurt Philip."

"Perhaps not," agreed the Comte cordially. "But Lady Mary can, as I think you will agree. There is no wish she could express that Wyclyffe would not immediately seek to fulfill, and I have it in *my* power to make Lady Mary . . . well, shall I say, express that wish?"

A picture of Philip's tormented face flashed across Harriet's brain; his expression when he admitted to her that he had gambled deeply and lost—encouraged by Lady Mary. It was on the tip of her tongue to betray her shock that anyone could so callously make such a threat, but a quick glance at the Comte's shuttered face warned her of the folly of appealing for his clemency. He meant every word he said, Harriet could see that. With sudden insight she knew that he would have no compunction in sacrificing his mistress, should that prove necessary. Useless to hope, then, that he would have compassion on Philip.

"You surely cannot mean to ruin Philip?" she suggested uneasily, but she knew both her expression and her voice betrayed her.

"You are not that naive, Miss Willoughby."

The cool voice held a sardonic inflection Harriet remembered from their other encounters.

"No," Harriet agreed soberly. "I agree it is useless to point out to you that Philip is a boy, deep in the throes of his first love affair, or that he might be pitied for his involvement with the woman you have made your mistress!" She flung back her head and looked straight into the Comte's indifferent eyes. "It is useless to plead for mercy, or expect you to understand the failings of other men, for you are not as them, are you, Comte? You are unmerciful, unyielding, a creature of stone who even *thinks* only at the bidding of his French masters!"

174

Harriet knew she had gone too far when his fingers bit into her shoulders. She did not need to catch the smothered oath to know she had aroused the anger in those cold gray eyes. Her breath caught on a shudder. He would never listen to her now. And he had meant every word he said; he *would* destroy Philip. Harriet closed her eyes.

"No matter what you say to me, I know you are a spy," she told him defiantly. "From the moment you kissed me in the gardens of Carlton House I knew."

For the second time she had succeeded in stirring him out of his normal implacable calm. She could feel the force of his raggedly expelled breath against her skin.

"A kiss?" he exclaimed disbelievingly. "Are you trying to tell me you would condemn me on one kiss? I doubt there is a jury in the land that would convict me on *that* evidence."

"It does not matter," Harriet said recklessly. "I know, and I am only surprised you do not ask for the same token of my silence as you did when you posed as a humble smuggler."

The gray eyes narrowed dangerously.

"This time you have gone too far!"

Harriet was jerked against his chest before she could save herself, arms like bars of iron imprisoning her so that there was no hope of escape.

"So, Miss Willoughby! You account yourself something of an expert on the quality of kisses, do you? Let us see how you like these, then?"

In profile the arrogant face held all the grim

intent of a hawk about to swoop on its prey. Harriet gave a small moan of terror and struggled ineffectually against the arms that bound her to his hard, unyielding body.

The touch of the Comte's lips was a fiery brand, she thought light-headedly as long fingers circled her neck and forced her to keep still.

Later, despairingly, when he had forced her to suffer the full onslaught of his ice-cold anger, Harriet knew nothing could ever be the same again. Outwardly she remained calm and composed, but inside, her heart was bleeding from a thousand lacerations inflicted by the cold savagery of his kiss.

Compared with this, those others had been merely the teasing gestures of an adult to a precocious child. Too late now to weep bitterly for the protective veil that had been rent from her eyes. She was too drained, too *frozen* to even feel anger. All she wanted was to be gone from this place and to forget that she had ever known a person called the Comte de la Valle.

"If I give you my promise to say nothing, will you see that no harm comes to Philip?" she asked dully.

"I shall ensure that no *further* harm comes to him," the Comte amended, "and certainly not at *my* hand, if that is what you mean."

"I shall not give you my promise until you tell me that you will free him from Lady Mary's influence," Harriet said without looking at him. "That is the price of my silence."

"How well you must love him," the Comte drawled. "The price of a good woman is above rubies, so the Bible would have us believe. Is that how he values you, or does he prefer the tawdry glitter of less worthy stones?"

He was sneering openly now, and Harriet cried out in pain, "Must you besmirch everything you touch? I shall not give you my promise until you give me yours."

"And I shall give you two days to come to your senses. If during that time you should be foolish enough to try to discredit me, your cousin will suffer."

Harriet tried to pull free of his restraining arms. She felt unbearably tired; a heavy weight, like some intolerable burden, seemed to have settled about her shoulders. If she could do nothing else, she would rescue Philip. Had it really only been twenty-four hours ago that she had so complacently savored the Comte's imminent downfall? She smiled pityingly for the girl she had been.

"Such a sombre face," murmured the Comte. "We must see if we cannot change that!"

Harriet flinched as his fingers touched her neck, and she knew by the sudden stillness of his body that he had guessed the reason why. The look she was coming to know and dread settled on his face.

"Afraid? We cannot have that. I had forgot you were so young. Shall I take away the nasty taste with something a little more pleasant?"

A warm flush mantled Harriet's cheeks, and she prayed he had not seen it. His rapid changes of mood baffled her. Now he was once again the urbane Frenchman, amused by her naivety, his manner bordering on the avuncular, but there was nothing avuncular about the expression in his eyes or the smile caught fleetingly by a shaft of moonlight.

"No, don't tremble," he whispered against her ear as his lips descended on hers for a second time.

Afterwards, when Harriet tried to recall her exact sensations, she could not. There was only a faint memory of piercing sweetness and a strange bittersweet awareness of everything about her adversary, as though every particle of her body had suddenly developed heightened sensitivity.

She was conscious of the measured thud of his heart against her breast; the swiftly indrawn breath as she tried desperately to avoid his lips; the totally unexpected tenderness of his touch; and the trembling awakening of her own heart to a danger far greater than any she had ever dreamed of knowing.

"There," he said when he released her. "Are you so sure now that you can recognize a man by his kisses, Miss Willoughby?"

When she only stared mutely up at him he said harshly, "Remember, you have two days to think it over—your silence in return for young Wyclyffe's safety."

chapter ten

Never had two days passed so swiftly. Harriet was in a constant fever of anxiety.

On the morning of her second day, Lady Phoebe took them to the Royal Academy, where the new season's offerings were being put on show.

Sophy was still walking about in a state of blissful euphoria, and when she did come down out of the clouds, it was only to murmur some inconsequentiality about the wedding.

Harriet was inspecting a charming watercolor of Cheyne Walk in Chelsea, admiring the artist's ability to catch the delightfully rural quality of the scene, when the Comte strolled in. He raised his quizzing glass to the landscape and

179

murmured approvingly, "Delightful. John Varley, he has a light touch."

For some reason the Comte's pronouncement obliged Harriet to smile very disparagingly indeed and agree that the landscape was pretty enough, if a little insipid!

"Sulking?" enquired the Comte dulcetly.

"No such thing," Harriet retorted. "Actually, I prefer portraits." It was a lie, but the Comte was not to know it. However, he appeared to be in an extremely quixotic humor, for he directed Harriet's attention to Thomas Lawrence's latest portrait of the Regent, which depicted the Prince in the full glory of one of his gold-doublooned uniforms, half a dozen Orders displayed prominently across his chest.

"Perhaps it is not the best example of his work," Harriet allowed stiffly, when they had both subjected the portrait to silent scrutiny.

Her eye strayed to another canvas—all sky and sea, but such colors!

"Turner," the Comte offered, following her gaze. "The combination of colors is quite unique in my opinion. That young man will go far."

"I am sure you did not seek me out merely to discuss the relative merits of the artists, sir," Harriet said formally.

"No indeed!" The Comte bestowed a fleeting smile on her. "Am I to take it you have come to a decision?"

No word of apology for his previous behavior, Harriet thought indignantly, no suggestion that he regretted that which had passed between them!

"Not yet," Harriet replied firmly, pointing out that she still had until that night to make her decision.

"But, of course," the Comte agreed urbanely. "Shall I see you tonight at Lady Fitzmartin's? I hear the *cantrice* who is to sing for us is most accomplished."

"My aunt has not yet decided about the invitation. Lady Fitzmartin is something of an eccentric, and Lady Phoebe has no wish to expose Sophy to vulgar curiosity with her betrothal so newly announced."

"Vulgar speculation, more like," corrected the Comte. "Tongues are already wagging at the speed with which she snatched up young Danvers once she realized his potential."

"Edward and Sophy have been in love for some considerable time," Harriet retorted with dignity.

"Indeed. But something tells me the love affair between Danvers and your aunt is considerably less long-standing," he murmured sardonically.

"What did *he* want?" Philip asked disagreeably a little later when the Comte had left.

Harriet sighed. Her cousin had changed. Gone was the boy she had once loved.

"He was just drawing my attention to the landscapes. How are things with you, Philip?"

He flushed, not pretending to misunderstand. "Not good," he admitted.

"Oh, Philip! Not more gambling?"

He turned on her, a mixture of anger and

shame mingled on his face. "Damn it all, Harriet, must you be so 'holier than thou'? Why shouldn't I gamble if I wish?"

"No reason," Harriet said unhappily, "but I cannot see what pleasure you gain from it when it makes you look ill and haggard. Surely there is no need?"

"Every need," Philip replied tersely. Only the previous evening Lady Mary had confided in him that several of her creditors were pressing. The Comte, she implied delicately, refused to support her now that she was enamoured of another man. Flattered, Philip had said naively that of course *he* must support her now.

At first she had demurred. She was vastly expensive, she warned; Philip was not a rich man. His pride stung, Philip had retorted that he might not be rich, but he had enough to buy whatever fripperies she wanted.

That had been before he saw the size of her dressmaker's bill! And there were others!

"Never mind," she had said gaily. She knew a way they could recoup their losses and have enough to fill their pockets as well.

The gaming house she had taken him to was in an alley off Piccadilly—a dimly lit place full of sunken-eyed people and the smell of sour wine. They had not won, of course. This time he had managed to regain his senses before he lost his ring again, but Mary had not been pleased. She had sulked all the way back to her house, dismissing him curtly on the doorstep and flouncing inside.

Harriet stared fearfully at him. "You mean . . ."

"I mean," Philip said rudely, "that if I am to keep Lady Mary in the fashion to which she is accustomed, I must take steps to improve my fortunes, and the only way I can do that is over the gaming tables."

He had not meant to put it so bluntly, and Harriet's white face caught him on the raw, but he would not retract the words now. His pride was sore, and his heart, too, and he regretted that he had been driven to vent his frustrations on his cousin.

Harriet looked around the Academy with a hunted expression. It was no use, and never had been, she admitted. She had no real choice. Philip must come first. She must seek out the Comte at the first opportunity and tell him she was ready to accede to his demands, galling though the thought was. She heard Lady Phoebe murmuring something about her plans for the evening and realized, with a sudden downward plunge of her heart, that her aunt did *not* intend to attend Lady Fitzmartin's evening party.

Perhaps the Comte was still somewhere in the Academy? Harriet searched frantically, but could not find him. An enquiry of Lady Burbridge elicited the information that he had had to return to his lodgings in Upper Brook Street.

There was nothing else for it, Harriet decided dismally. She would have to beard the lion in his den. Strange that she had once cautioned Sophy against visiting a man's rooms unchaperoned, and now here she was, about to commit exactly the same crime herself, although for vastly different reasons!

It had been easy for Harriet to extract from Lady Burbridge the information she wanted, but it was with a great deal of trepidation that she embarked upon her self-imposed task later in the day while Lady Phoebe and Sophy were engaged with Mrs. Fitch discussing the all-important matter of a bridal gown.

It was relatively simple to slip unnoticed from the house and, having decided that it would be foolish to court additional attention by walking alone through the streets of London, Harriet hailed a hackney and gave the jarvey her destination.

The carriage stopped outside an elegantly stuccoed house in Upper Brook Street, wedged between others of its kind and possessed of a certain degree of elegance.

Fortunately the street appeared to be deserted; not even a curtain twitched as Harriet marched up the immaculate steps and rapped on the knocker.

The butler—a well trained person, quite obviously—exhibited no surprise at being required to conduct her to his master's presence, instead declaring in lofty accents that the Comte was out.

Frustrated by this unexpected hitch in her plans, Harriet said energetically that in that case she would step inside and wait upon his return.

She half expected the butler to deny her access, but instead, back rigid with disapproval, he led Harriet to an elegantly furnished salon with the information that he would appraise the

Comte of her arrival immediately upon his return. Chastened by his obvious disapproval, Harriet sank into a chair.

The salon was comfortably furnished, if a little austere for Harriet's taste. Brocade-covered chairs dotted the room; a delicate porcelain figure reposed on a circular table with claw feet; and the Aubusson carpet faithfully echoed the muted greens and golds of the walls and ceiling. Long velvet draperies at the windows gave the promise of coziness when they were closed against the chill of evening. All in all, the room had a pleasingly restful appearance. This being the case, Harriet could not help wondering why *she* should feel so little benefit from her surroundings. The nervousness she had felt at the outset of her venture had increased steadily, until now she was starting at every unexpected sound, her nerves fluttering in agitated anxiety.

She was just chiding herself for her cowardice when she heard the outer door open and the sounds of someone's entry into the house.

"Where's that damned butler?" she heard the Comte say. "Fellow's never here when I want him. Never mind, we'll go into the salon!"

The salon! Harriet froze. That meant he was coming in here, and not alone! She must not be discovered, unchaperoned, in a bachelor gentleman's residence.

The door opened inward. Panicking, Harriet fled across the room, darting behind the velvet draperies at the very same moment as the Comte and his companion entered the salon.

From her hiding place she heard the chink

of a decanter against glasses and the Comte's drawl. "Shall we drink to the success of our mission?"

"It will be successful, then? I have been wanting to speak to you in private these few days past, but the opportunity has never presented itself. I take it the package will soon be in your hands?"

The Comte's visitor had a pleasant voice. He was no Frenchman, though; this man was English. The well-bred accents triggered off an illusive memory. Harriet tried to place it, straining to recall where she had heard the voice before, but the Comte was speaking again, and the memory vanished.

"I believe so. I have already received a message to the effect that it is available. A meeting has been arranged, although our friend has grown greedy. The price is more than we bargained for."

The man must be another of the Comte's fellow conspirators. A spy like himself! But what was the mysterious package of which they spoke? It was a puzzle too taxing for Harriet's weary brain.

It was suffocatingly warm behind the curtain, and her head was beginning to swim with the effort of holding her body rigidly still. If only she dared peer around the corner of the draperies, but common-sense cautioned her that to do so would be to court discovery.

Realizing that she had missed part of the conversation, Harriet heard the Comte's companion ask anxiously, "And our young friend.

Does she pose any real threat to you, do you think?"

"Miss Willoughby, you mean?" drawled the Comte. "You may safely leave that matter in my hands. The young lady is somewhat inclined to idealism," the Comte said cynically, "but I am sure she can be brought to see reason!"

Behind her protective curtain Harriet stiffened. How dare he sound so odiously confident? So sure that she would ultimately fall in with his plans? Apparently the other gentleman shared her view, for he asked doubtfully, "You mean you have threatened her in some fashion?"

"She is extremely attached to young Wyclyffe," the Comte said carelessly. "I believe he will prove to be the lever I need."

"So sure, Charles. Is there nothing you would not sacrifice for the success of this mission?"

There was a silence, and Harriet could almost picture the Comte's sardonic expression. He would be smiling with that touch of mockery she knew so well. She clenched her hands, wishing circumstances had not driven her to take this course. She felt rather than saw the Comte's expressive shrug.

"We are not playing a game. Sometimes it is necessary to be ruthless. Which is more important? Miss Willoughby's sensibilities, or a satisfactory conclusion to the matter we have labored over for so long?"

The other gentleman still seemed doubtful. Harriet heard him murmur, "Still, I wish there could have been another way."

He sounded far kinder than the Comte,

Harriet reflected. Surely he would never have placed her in such an intolerable position? Perhaps she was foolish to expect consideration from her enemies. Dust tickled her nose, and she longed to sneeze. She moved slightly and the curtain billowed. Had they seen her? She held her breath, but nothing happened. No determined footsteps hurried in the direction of her hiding place.

The gentleman moved closer to the door. Harriet heard the Comte say something in an undertone she could not quite catch. Several moments later there was the sound of a door opening and footsteps receding across the hall.

Shakily Harriet let out her breath. They had gone. Now all she had to do was quit the house unobserved. If there was any fairness in life, she reflected crossly, the fates would arrange matters now so that the Comte left with his visitor, thus enabling her to slip away undetected.

Several seconds elasped without the return of the Comte. Relieved, Harriet stretched her cramped limbs, only to freeze again as she heard the door opening.

Again there was the faint clinking of glass against glass, the squeak of springs as someone settled into a chair. It *must* be the Comte. What was she to do now, Harriet thought desperately. She could hardly emerge from behind the curtain and reveal her presence. She bit her lip thinking frantically. If only the Comte would leave! Perhaps when he had finished his wine . . .

Her whole body was aching with the effort

of keeping motionless. A rustle from the salon told her that the Comte was still there. No doubt stretching his legs out before the fire, she thought enviously. It was no use, she would have to do something.

"You can come out now, Miss Willoughby, unless you intend to remain there all night, although I can hardly suppose you to be comfortable!"

Harriet nearly jumped out of her skin. She started and trembled convulsively.

"Well, Miss Willoughby? Are you going to emerge, or must I be put to the trouble of fetching you? Such shyness is hardly in accord with your previous behavior, you know!" The dulcet tones only increased her chagrin.

She hovered indecisively behind the curtain for another second, heard the unmistakable sound of the Comte rising from his chair and hastily stepped out of her concealment, defiance writ large upon her troubled countenance.

"So. It seems you have decided to fight fire with fire," the Comte said softly. "I trust you found our conversation interesting?"

"Most illuminating," Harriet said through gritted teeth, "but I did *not* come here to spy upon you." With a fair imitation of the Comte's own derisive smile, she returned to the attack. "Such activities I leave to you, and others of your breed."

"A breed that is as far beneath you as the earth beneath the sun, eh?" the Comte suggested evenly. "Come, Miss Willoughby, I have no wish to trade insults with you. If you did not come to spy upon me, what are you doing in my salon?"

This was going to be harder than Harriet had imagined. When she had launched into her contemptuous attack upon him, she had forgotten that ultimately she would have to humble herself to beg his aid.

Stammering and stumbling a little over the explanation, she told him her story. The Comte listened in silence, thoughtfully swirling the contents of his wineglass, one arm resting negligently on the mantel, while the gray eyes studied the animated little face raised to his own.

"So, am I to take it, then, that you have changed your mind and are now prepared to accept my terms?"

Ignoring the sarcastic elevation of his eyebrows, Harriet said firmly, "Only if you give me your word that Lady Mary will terminate her association with Philip."

"Do you hope he will turn to you? I think not. Besides, he is a man, isn't he? What makes you so sure I shall be able to put an end to the connection?"

"I do not think Lady Mary would be interested in Philip if you did not neglect her," Harriet said simply, hoping her blushes would not betray her. This was not a subject she should be discussing, but her anxiety for Philip overruled all the precepts of maidenly modesty!

The Comte stared at her with narrowed eyes. "Are you suggesting that I should deliberately encourage Lady Mary's affections so that she will desert your cousin?" he asked incredulously. "A very pretty rogue you must think me, indeed!"

"I cannot see that it is any worse than what you have already done," Harriet said defensively.

"No?" The Comte's expression betrayed his disbelief. He turned his back on Harriet and seemed engrossed in a study of the fire. When he turned round again, his face was unreadable, his voice unusually clipped as he said shortly, "I trust your cousin is appreciative of the steps you would have me take on his behalf, but are you so sure Lady Mary will welcome me back in her bed?"

Harriet flinched, as much at the derisive expression in his eyes as at the frankness of his words. Her chin jutted forward. Well, she too could speak plainly, unladylike though it undoubtedly was!

"I have heard it said that Lady Mary has expensive tastes. I am sure she will recognize that you are far better equipped to indulge them than my cousin is!"

For a moment she was almost frightened by the anger leaping to life in the Comte's eyes.

"Quite a set-down, Miss Willoughby," he said tightly. "However, you have not yet convinced me. Still, I shall make a bargain with you. I shall do what I can to free your besotted cousin from Lady Mary's toils, in return for your word that you say nothing about what you have learned of me, and . . ."

"And what?" Harriet asked apprehensively.

The Comte seemed to consider her, his eyes moving from her face to the slender body inside the lemon walking dress, until Harriet's heart was beating with slow, painful strokes. A sudden sensation of breathlessness overcame her.

"Do not look at me so . . ." she whispered, her hand creeping up to her throat as though she would still the frantic pulse that had begun to beat there.

"Like what?" asked the Comte softly. "Come, answer me. You have not shrunk from frankness on previous occasions, so do not pretend now that *I* am the cause of those blushes!"

Harriet, rooted to the spot, trembled. This was the Comte in a mood she had never seen before; a reckless, dangerous mood when even his voice seemed to have taken on a new seductive quality she had never heard before but which sent small quivers of alarm along her nerves.

"I seem to recollect upon the occasion of our last meeting you had cause to mention the quality of my kisses," the Comte said thoughtfully, ignoring Harriet's small gasp. "At that time I endeavored to show you that a man has many sides; perhaps the lesson should be completed?"

He had crossed the space between them with two lithe strides before Harriet had even had time to assimilate his words. She shuddered as he smiled mirthlessly down into her face.

"Never mind," he told her softly, "you can always tell yourself it is for Wyclyffe's sake that you endure my embrace. I trust he will be properly appreciative!"

"Haven't you already p-p-punished me enough?" Harriet stammered nervously. "I cannot see what subjecting me to further insult will achieve."

"No?" drawled the Comte suavely. "But then, you see, Miss Willoughby, even the best of us are not infallible. Suffice it to say that I have my reasons, and they are enough to assure me that I must . . . er . . . inflict this additional warning."

As he spoke, he bent his head to trap the betraying pulse of her neck, and at his touch Harriet was assailed by the strangest sensation.

Oddly weak, she could only murmur an incoherent protest when the Comte's lips brushed her own, her eyes seeking his fearfully and wondering at the glinting satisfaction momentarily apparent in the gray depths, no longer cold, but warm, so warm that she caught her breath in wonder, her last coherent thought she must be dreaming, for surely there was no other explanation for the look she had seen on the Comte's face, nor for her own instinctive response to it.

She knew she should feel degraded, and humiliated by the determined pressure of that alien mouth, but instead a sweetness beyond any reason ran through her veins like melting honey. Her lips parted beneath the mastery of the Comte's. He sighed, half in triumph, half in despair. Harriet felt as though the whole world had turned upside down and she no longer knew right from wrong. She only knew that she wanted to remain forever in the Comte's arms, savoring the intoxicating bliss of his lips on hers.

Even as she formed the thought, shocked

denial ran through her. She stiffened, and instantly the Comte released her. He moved back to the table and poured himself another glass of wine, his hand perfectly steady. No betraying tremor marked his voice, but Harriet had the unassailable conviction that he had not meant to kiss her as he had.

Had he for one moment imagined he held Lady Mary's lissome body in his arms? The thought was strangely painful. Trembling with reaction, Harriet subsided into a chair. A nameless longing, totally alien and instantly suppressed, seemed to have taken possession of her body.

"I think it is time you left, Miss Willoughby," the Comte said curtly. "I shall do what I can for your cousin."

"And you have my word that I shall not betray you," Harriet managed to say proudly, before she fled.

All the way back to South Audley Street, she kept picturing his face, the curious look she had surprised in the depths of his eyes, as though something long slumbering had wakened to life. Something that by no stretch of the imagination could have been aroused by her! Odd that such a thought, instead of being reassuring, should only have the most lowering effect upon her spirits.

It was not possible that England's enemy could have practiced even greater treachery than she had imagined and stolen something else besides Lord Burbridge's military secrets, was it?

Harriet was very much afraid it was, and

since the article in question could be of no possible use to the Comte, she was inclined to think he had knowingly purloined it just to reinforce the intelligence that he was a foe she could not hope to vanquish!

chapter eleven

Harriet had hoped that the Comte's intervention would put a swift end to Philip's involvement with Lady Mary. Heartsore, she
acknowledged that no woman could prefer the
attentions of her cousin to those of the Frenchman, especially not a woman of Lady Mary's
caliber. However, her hopes were dashed when
Philip called at South Audley Street one morning
and begged Harriet to accompany him in his
curricle for a ride in the Park.

Dismayed and alarmed, as much by his
worn expression as by his desire to see her alone,
Harriet complied.

South Audley Street was all abustle with
preparations for the wedding—now grown somewhat from the original small affair. Edward had

recently returned from a visit to his grandfather's
estate and was full of the preparations going
forward on the suite of rooms the Marquis had
placed at the young people's disposal.

Lady Phoebe had wanted the ceremony to
take place at St. George's Hanover Square, but
Sir George had put his foot down. Sophy was to
be married by his brother-in-law, and the same
church that had seen so many Wyclyffe marriages celebrated should now see another.

Harriet hoped she was not an envious
cousin, but somehow whenever she observed
Sophy's happiness, an enormous lump would rise
in her throat, and she would be overcome by a
stupid inclination to burst into tears. Moreover,
on those occasions when she pictured her father's
small church—occasions which were more numerous than she could find reasonable explanation
for—it was not Sophy and Edward she pictured
kneeling together before her Papa, but herself
and a gentleman who bore a strange resem-
blance to the Comte.

Harriet was obliged to take herself seriously
to task for this weakness, but it was all to no
avail. For this reason she welcomed Philip's
company. The sight of his troubled face would
remind her of all the Comte's many failings,
chief amongst which, for some totally mystify-
ing reason, was not his activities as an admitted
enemy of her country, but the promptitude with
which he had agreed to resume his relationship
with Lady Mary.

It was useless for Harriet to tell herself that
she was a fool and worse, for treasuring those
few fleeting seconds in his arms, when he had

kissed her with passion and tenderness, or to remind her susceptible heart that his love—if that cynical heart admitted the existence of such an emotion—was given to another, Harriet still daydreamed of how things might have been had they met in different circumstances.

On this occasion, there was no Honorable Toby to break the uncomfortable silence that had sprung up between them from the moment Philip handed Harriet into his curricle.

"Harriet, I have to talk to someone, otherwise I believe I shall go mad," Philip said suddenly.

"Is it . . . is it Lady Mary?" Harriet asked on a wave of foreboding. Had the Comte already made good his promise?

"Yes, it is," Philip replied bleakly. "She has given me my *congé*. Thrown me over for de la Valle. I suppose I should have been prepared for it—she never made any secret of the fact that she found him attractive—and his wealth more so," Philip told her bitterly. "I will not criticize her now for the honesty that is so much a part of her."

But Harriet knew that under the clipped words lay a vast oasis of pain.

"Philip . . ." She touched his arm commiseratingly, startled when he jerked away from her.

"Don't . . . don't tell me I shall forget her, or that I am better off without her. God, Harriet, I swear I cannot live without her."

"But if she has given you your *congé*," Harriet said slowly, "if she truly prefers the Comte—"

"The Comte! It is not him she loves, but his money. Well, I too can give her that and something else, too—something the Comte will never give her."

Seriously alarmed, Harriet stared into her cousin's set face. "You, Phillip? But you have no money . . ."

"I can get it," Philip said rigidly. "The town is full of money-lenders ready to offer money against a man's soul if the rates are usorious enough. My father cannot live forever, and once the estate is mine—"

"Philip, no!" Harriet cried, horrified. "You cannot mean what you are saying!"

"I do mean it," Philip said stubbornly. "I shall borrow against my inheritance, and then I shall offer Lady Mary my fortune and my hand."

"*Marriage?*" stammered Harriet. "Oh, Philip, no! Your mama—"

"I must live my own life, Harriet, not the life others would choose for me."

It was plain, Harriet thought, that Philip was in no mood to see reason. His passion for Lady Mary had blinded him to everything but his need for her. Had *she* perhaps precipitated this crisis by asking the Comte to interfere between them? If so, she now had a responsibility to ensure that Philip did not pursue his proposed course. Harriet believed unshakably that were he allowed to marry Lady Mary, it would be a short path to disillusionment and thence to despair and regret. It could not be allowed to happen; it *would* not be allowed to happen, not while she was able to stop it, but what could she do?

On the way back to South Audley Street they passed the Comte's curricle, the Comte controlling the four excitable Arabs that pulled it with an ease that was the envy of less accomplished gentlemen.

Seated beside him in a gown of amber crape was Lady Mary, oblivious to anyone but the man at her side. The picture should have afforded her satisfaction, Harriet knew that. Why, then, did she feel suddenly bereft, deprived, conscious of the loss of something infinitely precious and totally irreplacable!

If she had needed any further confirmation of her cousin's infatuation for Lady Mary, Harriet had it in the blind, anguished gaze he turned upon the Comte's curricle, his face paper white, the knuckles shining through his skin where his hands gripped the reins.

As they waited for a crossing sweeper to make way for them, Harriet heard a passer-by comment *sotto voce*, to his female companion, "There goes de la Valle with La Belle Mary. I thought it wasn't possible to rake over dead ashes."

"Where the *lady* is concerned," the lady replied tartly, "the fire was never doused!"

The couple were gone before Harriet could hear any more, but the words rang unpleasantly in her head long after Philip had deposited her on his mama's doorstep, refusing an invitation to come in with her and partake of a glass of wine and some sweet biscuits.

It was only later, alone in her bedchamber,

pacing that small room with nervous impatience, that Harriet managed to banish the Comte from her mind and instead concentrate on a means of rescuing Philip from the self-destruction upon which he was set.

Only after the beginnings of a headache had caused her to cease her perambulations did a solution occur to Harriet, but one so foolhardy, so fraught with danger and risk that Harriet went cold even to contemplate it!

If she could not appeal to Philip, she reasoned, then could she not instead appeal to the lady? She was quite sure Lady Mary had not the slightest desire to marry her cousin. The way she had been looking at the Comte had confirmed Harriet's own secret conviction that had their roles been reversed, and the Comte been penniless, Lady Mary would have forgone wealth to be with him. No, if she was to save Philip she must appeal directly to Lady Mary. A clean cut, however painful, would heal faster than a series of lesser blows. Lady Mary was a woman, after all. Surely she would listen to Harriet's pleas and set Philip free, especially now, when she had all that her heart desired?

It was a reckless, desperate stratagem, but what real alternative did she have? Harriet stared at the wall, delicately papered in a trelliswork of roses. She had no choice. She must save Philip! He was the brother she had never had, the companion of her childhood. A small, fluttering sigh broke from her lips. In a dream she rang for her maid. The servants knew everything. From her she would learn Lady Mary's direction. She would go after dinner when Lady

Phoebe and Sophy would be engaged in preparations for the wedding.

The succulent fish dish might have been so much sawdust, Harriet reflected, as she forced another forkful down a throat tight with tension. She was conscious of giving vague answers to Sophy's excited chatter, and once or twice surprised a considering look in Lady Phoebe's eyes. Her aunt must not guess what she intended, Harriet thought desperately, as she forced herself to appear natural.

The meal seemed to last for an eternity. Never had Harriet been so relieved to rise from the table. The glib lie that slipped from her tongue when she told her aunt of her "headache" shamed her, but it was a necessary subterfuge, although it did not help Harriet's sensitive conscience when Sophy offered to come and sit with her so that she should not feel lonely. Assuring her cousin that she would recover faster alone, Harriet made her escape.

The maid, who believed herself to be assisting at some romantic escapade, was waiting for Harriet in her room, a heavy opera cloak laid out on the bed.

"No one will ever recognize you in this, miss," she assured Harriet. "Jem has a hackney waiting by the backstairs, and I'll wait up to let you in."

Inwardly quaking, Harriet followed the girl down the narrow servants' stairs at the back of the house, her heart in her mouth lest they be discovered.

It was dark and cold in the street when the

maid pushed open the door. Harriet had never ventured out alone at night before, and she was trembling a little, despite her attempts to appear collected. Rather hesitantly she stepped into the carriage, giving the man Lady Mary's direction. Over and over she repeated the words she intended to say to Lady Mary, her hands unconsciously clasped together in an attitude of supplication.

As Lady Phoebe never sat down to dinner before eight o'clock, Harriet judged that it could not be far off ten when the hackney rattled to a standstill outside Lady Mary's small villa.

Paying off the man, she stepped down, looking all about her. The street was deserted, and since it did not benefit from the new gas lights, the long shadows gave it a rather menacing aspect. Squaring her shoulders, Harriet approached the door. Not a glimmer of light showed through the heavy curtains pulled across the windows. She lifted the knocker.

When no one answered her summons, Harriet tried again. To her amazement, the door swung open under her touch. A thin shaft of light showed under one of the doors. Confused, Harriet wondered what to do. Where were the servants?

At last she stepped inside, half expecting to be confronted by an irate footman. She seemed to be making a habit of visiting people unannounced.

To her own apprehensive ears the sound of her shoes across the tiled floor seemed very loud, but no one appeared to question her right to enter Lady Mary's house unannounced.

A little timidly Harriet opened the door under which she had seen the light. It was quite empty. She stared around rather blankly. Where *was* everyone?

From the doorway the very last voice she had expected to hear drawled softly, "Dear me, Miss Willoughby! You *do* seem to have the knack of turning up in the most unlikely places, don't you? Now what brings you here, I wonder? Ah, yes, young Wyclyffe, perchance?"

"Comte . . ." Harriet faltered, ignoring his allusion to the reason for her presence.

The Comte walked farther into the room. Harriet thought he looked rather pale, but he was as nonchalant as ever, one hand tucked casually inside his jacket.

"What are *you* doing here?" Even as the words left her lips, Harriet blushed. In her surprise at finding him here, she had overlooked his relationship with Lady Mary.

"Not what you quite obviously suppose, *ma fille*," the Comte mocked, "but I could ask you the same question, you know."

"Where is Lady Mary?" Harriet asked, ignoring him.

He smiled rather faintly. "I believe at this very moment she is on her way to France, Miss Willoughby, taking with her the pickings she made from those young fools amongst whom your cousin so nearly numbered." He spoke almost abstractly, as though Lady Mary's departure were of no more moment than that of a mere acquaintance. Confused, Harriet looked at him, trying to penetrate the laconic barrier of his mockery to discover what he was really thinking. If it was true and Lady Mary had gone to France, she had come on a wasted journey; Philip was safe.

"Why did you not go with her?" she asked curiously. "There can be nothing to keep you in England now!"

"You think not? Is it completely beyond the bounds of comprehension that I might have some unfinished business which keeps me here?"

As he spoke he was watching Harriet intently. She felt confused—as much by his words as the way he was regarding her. With an effort she pulled herself together.

"I suppose you mean more spying?"

The accusation fell rather weakly on her own ears, and the Comte seemed far from impressed.

"And if I were to say it was something else?"

"I wouldn't believe you!" Her breath seemed to catch in her throat; there was a feeling of tense expectancy in the air.

"Little fool!" The words were a caress. Harriet trembled on the brink of a startling discovery—what had happened to her much-vaunted desire to see the Comte brought low?

"Harriet!"

Neither of them had heard Philip come in. He stared at the frozen tableau, frowning heavily. "Harriet, what's going on here?"

"Not what you so obviously suppose, Wyclyffe," the Comte drawled, answering for her. "And we might ask you the same question."

Philip flushed uncomfortably. He had not been able to forget Harriet's stricken face when he told her of his plans. Conscience had warred with desire ever since, and the chance meeting with an old acquaintance had brought home to him the perils of his situation. The young man had been involved with Lady Mary himself and had not been slow to warn Philip not to get caught in the same trap. In the end, conscience had won; his infatuation had been a midsummer madness, but now it was over. He had come to tell Lady Mary so, and take his leave of her. The last thing he had expected to be confronted with was his cousin in the company of Lady Mary's one-time lover.

"I have come to see Lady Mary," he said stiffly. "Harriet, you should not be here—"

"I suspect it was on your behalf that she came, Wyclyffe," the Comte interrupted. "Is that not so, Miss Willoughby?" Without waiting for Harriet's reply, he added sardonically, "You are fortunate in your relatives. As Miss Willoughby will confirm, Lady Mary is no longer with us."

Philip glanced helplessly at Harriet. "What is he talking about?"

"I'm afraid it's true, Philip. Lady Mary has been selling secret information to the French. She has left for France." Here was her opportunity to add that the Comte, too, was involved in that same treachery. Involuntarily, she glanced up at him. He was completely motionless, his eyes fixed on her face. A trembling surge of pain shot through her. Her mouth had gone quite dry. She *must* tell Philip! Wrenching her eyes away from the Comte's, she turned to her cousin.

"Philip . . ."

A faint gasp from the Comte brought her eyes back to his face. He had gone dreadfully pale, small beads of sweat on his forehead. To her horror, he swayed slightly, his eyes closing.

"Philip!"

Alerted by her warning, Philip sprang forward just in time to catch the Comte as he fell.

All thoughts of revenge forgotten, Harriet flew to his side, kneeling down next to the inert figure, her skirts spread about her like the pale wings of a moth.

"What's wrong with him?" she asked urgently.

In the very moment of her victory she had realized the truth. She had not exposed the Comte, because she *could* not. She looked into his white face, waiting anxiously while Philip slipped his hand under his jacket. He grimaced, withdrawing it quickly.

"He's been shot, high up in the shoulder. He's losing blood fast." His voice grew rough. "The fool, what did he mean by standing there talking when all the time he knew . . ." He saw Harriet blanch and compressed his lips. "Don't *you* faint. We'll have to do something to help him, but he can't be found here, not when Lady Mary's treachery becomes known. What was he doing here, anyway?"

Her hesitation was only momentary. Ruthlessly ignoring all claims of loyalty and right, Harriet shrugged her shoulders.

"Perhaps he was trying to persuade Lady Mary to stay." She saw her cousin's face and touched his arm lightly, "I'm sorry about that, Philip."

"Perhaps it is for the best. I had come to tell her it was all over between us. I've been a fool, I know, but at least it is not too late to mend matters. But now we had best see to the Comte. . . ."

"We could take him back to his lodgings and call a doctor," Harriet suggested.

Philip glanced consideringly at the unconscious man. "I can't tell whether the bullet is still lodged in his shoulder. I wonder how it happened?"

It was a question Harriet had been asking herself. She bit her lip, guiltily aware that she had not told Philip the full truth. How sympathetic would he be to the Comte's plight if he knew that he was a spy?

"Harriet, he's coming round!"

Distracted, she stared at the Comte. He opened his eyes, focusing on her face. "So, am I completely discovered now, *ma belle?*"

A warm tide of color swept Harriet's face.

"I think he's rambling," Philip muttered. "Comte, who shot you?"

The Comte gave a ghost of his former sardonic smile. "Why, Lady Mary, of course, who else?"

Philip blanched, both men ignoring Harriet's shocked protest.

"She took exception to my refusal to fall in with her plans. . . . I . . ."

"He's gone again. Help me lift him up, Harriet; between us we can perhaps get him to his lodgings. If he lives that long," he added grimly.

In repose the saturnine face looked oddly

vulnerable. She was a sentimental idiot, Harriet chided herself. Why on earth hadn't she exposed him? The dark hair lay untidily against his forehead. His eyelashes were long and thick, feathering the pale skin. Harriet's heart turned over with melting tenderness. What was happening to her? She suspected that she knew the answer, but mercifully the Comte's plight prevented her from dwelling upon it.

Between them she and Philip got him to his feet, supporting his inert body between them.

There was a touch of frost in the air, and Harriet shivered a little in the cold night air. One or two strollers stared incuriously at the strange trio but no one made any attempt to apprehend them. Possibly they mistook them for revellers.

Upper Brook Street was gained without incident, although the Comte was shivering violently, his arm a dead weight about Harriet's shoulders. A sleepy-eyed footman opened the door to them, his eyes widening as he beheld his master.

"The Comte has been attacked by footpads," Philip informed him tersely. "You had best send for a doctor."

They had decided on this explanation on the way, Philip expressing the view that it would save a lot of unnecessary questions. He was badly shaken by the Comte's revelations about Lady Mary's activities, although they had served to disperse his last lingering longing for her.

Carefully he and Harriet placed the Comte upon a sofa—in the very same room that had been the scene of Harriet's earlier confrontation with him.

"I had best go and find his valet. When the doctor arrives he will need help, and they had best have some brandy on hand, as well."

Harriet paled at his grim tone.

"Will he live, do you think?"

Two hours ago her one desire in life had been to see him unmasked; now she could think of nothing but the agony of soul his death would cause her.

"I don't know." Philip looked very serious. "It all depends on his own determination to live." He looked at Harriet's set face, cursing his ineptitude. He had always had the impression that she did not care overmuch for the Comte. Now he could see that he was mistaken.

"He has a strong constitution," he comforted her clumsily. "Stay here with him, while I go and find his valet."

Harriet could not sit still. She looked helplessly into the Comte's unguarded face as though she could find the answer to her own dilemma there. She had committed a dreadful crime; she was actually aiding a criminal to evade justice, but she felt not a single pang of guilt.

The Comte's eyelashes fluttered. He struggled to sit up, hectic patches of color staining his cheeks. "Well, Miss Willoughby, are you satisfied now? When am I to expect the runners?"

Harriet winced, unable to bear the thought of his being taken into custody by the Bow Street Runners.

"You must not talk. You are losing a lot of blood." Without thinking, she knelt at his side, ripping a flounce from her petticoat to stanch the wound. Fingers trembling, she leant across him.

"Second thoughts?" he jeered, his jaw clenching suddenly. Pain etched white lines around his mouth.

"You must not talk," Harriet whispered. "I have said nothing to Philip. You must get well and leave the country before you are discovered!"

She heard his indrawn breath, saw his eyes blazing with sudden, inexplicable emotion. He was flushed, quite obviously feverish, but as Harriet placed the lawn pad against his shoulder he recoiled, a savage imprecation jerking past his closed lips.

"Did I hurt you?" She faltered, withdrawing her hand.

The Comte lay back, his eyes closed. "Is it really true, that you have said *nothing*?"

Flushing at his incredulous tone, Harriet nodded her head, not willing to risk speech, lest she disgrace herself utterly by bursting into tears. His eyes flew open. His good arm closed about her and drew her against his chest. "God, *Harriet!*"

It was the first time he had used her name, and tears stung her eyes at her own weakness. He buried his face in the smooth hollow of her neck, pressing feverish kisses against her frail bones and murmuring incoherent phrases.

Against all reason, a wild tide of sweetness flooded through her. Instead of repulsing him, her arms crept up to hold him protectively, cradling the dark head. From a great distance she heard his muted curse and felt the shudder that wracked his body as he lifted his mouth and found hers. Gone was the cool, laconic facade. His hands trembled as they touched her hair, and Harriet heard him mutter, "Your Philip cannot deny me this, Harriet, for it is only just that I take payment for the service I have rendered him! You have undermined all my defenses and left me helpless, *ma belle;* your compassion is a thousand times more dangerous than your anger, did you know that?"

Harriet could say nothing. She could only feel the bittersweetness that his touch aroused. Even as he kissed her, she knew his strength was fading, and when Philip came hurrying back into the room, he had lapsed into a fever, muttering unintelligibly under his breath, while she tried to stem the red tide on which he was slipping away from her.

"Lady Mary must have left him for dead," Philip told her. "God, Harriet, how could I ever have let myself be so bemused by her? What manner of woman must she be to do *this?*"

It hurt her to remember how he had stood and talked with her, all the time his fingers pressing tightly on the wound that must, even then, have been causing him exquisite agony. And she had thought him a posturing dandy.

"You must have only missed Lady Mary's departure by minutes," Philip continued. "I thank God for that, at least. If you had interrupted her . . ."

She, too, would probably have shared the Comte's fate. Almost disinterestedly she considered the thought. Tonight had held so many shocks that her brain seemed incapable of feeling any more.

The arrival of the doctor took Philip from the room while he gave an edited version of what had happened. He came back a few minutes later, taking Harriet's arm.

"You must leave without being seen. The servants will keep the doctor in the library until we are gone. We had best go now. I should hate Mama to discover that you are missing."

She gave a last despairing look at the Comte's inert figure before she allowed Philip to draw her out of the room.

In the street she watched the house with tortured eyes. "It is over, Harriet," Philip said softly. "It is out of our hands now. We must both forget!"

Later that evening, back in her bedroom, she stared sightlessly in front of her. It made no sense; fate had handed her a golden opportunity to be revenged upon the Comte, and instead of taking it, she . . . Why? Without thought for her own country, she had sought to aid a man whom she knew to be a traitor. Fixedly Harriet stared into the darkness. In this case, the traitor was her own heart. Love had made a mockery of her determination to see the Comte brought to justice; love had wrought the change in her feelings. The feminine heart was an unpredictable organ; never had she dreamed that hers would desert her for an enemy of her country. Slow tears slid down her cheeks, falling unheeded onto her pillow as she contemplated a future without the Comte.

Three days later, Philip walked into his mama's drawing room while Harriet was bent over a letter to her parents.

The news of Lady Mary's disappearance was all over London. Some said she had fled with a lover, others that she had gone searching for a new one. No one seemed to have guessed the truth.

The other chief topic of conversation was a supposed "duel" between the Comte de la Valle and an unknown person. Naturally the whole world was agog to learn the reason for the "duel," but since no one could discover the identity of the second combatant, and the Comte was still confined to his bedchamber, the curious were having to exercise their imaginations to supply the missing details. It was commonly held that the cause of the quarrel could only have been a lady, and speculation was rife as to the identity of the lucky recipient of the Comte's attentions.

When she at last managed to get Philip to herself, Harriet could barely bring herself to ask the all-important question.

She found Philip strangely reluctant to discuss the matter, evasive almost, merely tendering the information that thus far the Comte still clung to life, but that was all.

Harriet, who had longed to know whether perhaps he had asked for her in any moment of lucidity, had to swallow the question and wonder a little bitterly if she would ever learn to come to terms with the love that threatened to destroy all her hard-won peace of mind.

With each passing day, her longing for the

Comte intensified so that there was never a moment when she was not conscious of her loss. Those few moments in his arms had been no more than the reactions of a fevered man who would have reacted so to any woman who had offered him tenderness, and yet Harriet knew she would gladly give up her right to eternal life for the bittersweet joy of experiencing them again!

chapter twelve

Autumn lay on the Marsh like a gray blanket. The few stunted trees had long since lost the last of their leaves, and frost crackled underfoot among the browning reeds.

It seemed to Harriet that nature reflected her own mood, although unlike the earth, her life lay barrenly before her for countless empty years. For her there could be no spring, no renewal of hopes and love.

She had left London without seeing the Comte again. Rumor whistled around the streets like an April breeze; some said he was already dead; others that he lay wracked on a bed of fever and pain; but whenever Harriet tried to discover the truth, she came up against a blank wall.

She had even toyed with the idea of visiting the house in Upper Brook Street yet again, to glean what little information she could, but on the one occasion she managed to pluck up the courage to walk past, the blinds were down over the windows and the knocker off the door, signifying that no one was in residence.

Philip knew as little as she did herself, and Harriet could only hope that the Comte had recovered sufficiently to quit the country, for the safety of France. Lord and Lady Burbridge were gone on a visit to Lord Burbridge's country estate, and Harriet wondered whether Lord Burbridge had had any suspicions that his young friend was not all that he seemed. Once she would have longed for this to be the case; now she found herself praying that it was not.

Before their London visit had terminated and the Burbridges themselves had left town, Lord Burbridge had called at South Audley Street, proffering the information that his secretary had left him and asking Lady Phoebe if she thought Philip might be interested in the post.

Naturally Lady Phoebe had been overjoyed, and so had Philip. Half a dozen more years would see him comfortably settled in the country, bringing up a promising family of his own, especially if he were to meet some suitable young heiress through Lord Burbridge's good offices. The thought affected Harriet not one whit. The brief summer madness that had led her to attribute to Philip all the virtues of a Knight of old was gone forever, and in its place had come the knowledge of real love—an emotion that owed nothing to circumstance or convention. Deep within her heart, Harriet knew that she would sacrifice everything she had ever held dear if only the Comte were to come to her again.

The celebrations for the Regency continued, but for Harriet they had lost their savor. She could never enter a ballroom without hoping to see the familiar dark head and the mockingly raised eyebrow, but always it was in vain.

The mournful cry of a moorhen jerked her back to the present. Only that morning a gilt-edged invitation and a long, much-crossed letter had arrived from Sophy, now firmly established as a Marchioness.

The old Marquis had not lasted long after the death of his favorite grandson. He had lost the will to live, his doctor said. Hardly had the marriage taken place, with Harriet an ethereal bridesmaid in palest lemon silk, than the Captain had been called upon to take up the mantle of responsibility doffed by his grandfather.

This was not the first time Harriet had received a pressing invitation to visit her cousin, but this time Sophy had a special reason for writing. It seemed she was to give a Christmas ball, although technically speaking, they were still in black for the late Marquis. "A family affair," Sophy called it gaily—Lord and Lady Burbridge, her parents, Philip (if he could be spared from his duties), Harriet herself, and perhaps one of two near neighbors.

As a postscript she added that Lord and Lady Burbridge were to bring a young gentleman from London—Lord Burbridge's godson, a gentleman who had recently been lauded by the Regent himself for his services to his country, and whom Sophy very much wished her to meet!

Harriet had come out onto the moor to be alone, away from her mama's anxious presence. Elizabeth Willoughby had watched her daughter with increasing concern ever since her return from London. With a mother's instinct she had not needed to be told what ailed Harriet, but when the weeks slipped by and summer gave way to autumn and Harriet still refused to talk about whatever troubled her, Elizabeth sighed and reflected that the child had given way to the woman, and the woman plainly asked no one to share the burden she carried.

She watched Philip's attentions to her daughter whenever he chanced to come home and wondered if Harriet guessed that he was halfway to falling in love with her. If she did, she gave no sign of it, treating him with a mixture of affection and indifference that drove him to reflect bitterly on the folly that had first taken him from her side.

Now with Sophy's letter on the vicarage mantel and her concern increasing rather than abating, Elizabeth Willoughby made up her mind that even if she had to neglect her responsibility to her husband and his parish, she would accompany Harriet to Upton to make sure she accepted Sophy's invitation.

While Harriet wandered the moor in search of solace, Mrs. Willoughby planned and plotted, with Lady Phoebe's encouragement. With Sophy off her hands and Lucy still in the schoolroom, Lady Phoebe had discovered a fondness for her niece she had never suspected, more so because that young lady was being so eminently sensible over Philip's budding infatuation.

For once the sisters-in-law found themselves with a common cause, and Lady Phoebe assured Harriet's mama that *she* would undertake to remove Harriet to Upton, whether her niece went willingly or no!

Wandering the Marsh engrossed in her own unhappy thoughts, Harriet relived her encounters with the Comte. If he were to appear today, materializing out of the thin veil of mist sweeping in from the sea, there was nothing on this earth that could prevent her from running into his arms. Was he thinking of her, wherever he was? Harriet shook her head over her own folly. Doubtless he had forgotten her very existence. Why was it, then, that her foolish heart kept on yearning, hoping that one day, somewhere, she would turn, see him, and know that her love was returned?

For once, Sir George seemed quite happy to leave his home. He rubbed his hands together with satisfaction, giving Harriet a hearty kiss on the cheek as she stepped into the carriage. He would ride on the box, he informed the ladies, thus affording them a little more room. "Affording *him* an opportunity to talk about hunting and horse-racing with the groom, more like!" Lady Phoebe said with a snort of exasperation, but she seemed well content to have her niece to herself. Sophy had written her that she believed she was "in an interesting condition," Lady Phoebe confided to Harriet, and she wanted to make sure that her daughter did not overdo things. Not when she might be carrying the future Marquis! Harriet hid a wan smile at this resurgence of the old Lady Phoebe.

When the carriage set them down outside the grim pile of gray stone that was Upton, Harriet saw at once that Sophy had taken on the bloom of a girl very much in love, who knows that her love is returned.

The party from the Marsh had barely put a foot inside the enormous hall before Sophy was whisking Harriet upstairs, leaving her parents in the care of her housekeeper.

She had given Harriet a room decorated in shades of green and silver overlooking the vast parkland where a lake glinted ice-blue under the thin winter sun.

"Edward says we shall have snow for Christmas," Sophy declared with satisfaction as she sank onto the bed, plainly intending to have a long talk with her cousin.

"Oh, Harriet, you cannot know how very pleasant it is to be married to someone you love," she confided naively, plainly about to enlarge upon this statement, until she saw her cousin's pale, haunted face and decided it would be best to converse on other, less evocative, subjects. "We have all manner of entertainments planned," she told Harriet. "Besides the ball, the gentlemen can hunt on Boxing Day." She pulled a wry face. "Of course, *I* cannot ride—but I make

221

no doubt that Mama will have told you of my hopes in *that* direction."

Sophy's delicately flushed cheeks told their own story, and Harriet, who had never until that moment begrudged her cousin any of her happiness, suddenly felt an unmistakable stab of jealousy.

Sophy chattered on, gaily unaware of Harriet's withdrawal. "Lord and Lady Burbridge arrived this morning, and of course, the Duke!"

"The Duke?" Harriet raised an eyebrow.

"You know, Harriet," Sophy explained hurriedly. "I wrote you about him. He is Lord Burbridge's godson. Is it not the most exciting thing? The Prince himself praised him for his gallantry, and Lady Burbridge told me he nearly lost his life! Don't you think he is wonderfully brave, for he had no need to place himself in such danger, you know, and it was only on account of his close relationship with Lord Burbridge that he accepted at all."

Harriet had the impression that Sophy was desperately trying to cover something up. She had always chattered on when she was nervous. She was just about to question her when Sophy embarked upon a further catalogue of the Duke's virtues.

"Only think! The most romantical story, rather like Edward's, really, for the Duke could have had no notion that *he* would inherit the title. His uncle and cousin contracted smallpox, you must know, and died within a sennight of each other. Vern was in the Peninsula at the time, so Lord Burbridge told me, and had to sell out. Wraxton Priory is the most lovely place,

Harriet, I'm sure you will love it! So much nicer than Upton, although Edward has promised me that if I give him a son, he will tear Upton down and rebuild it stone by stone just as I please."

Sophy gave an entirely feminine giggle at this piece of male nonsense, for none knew better than she just how devoted her husband was to the home of his ancestors. Indeed, there were moments when he came to the little sitting room she had made her very own, so bowed down with the cares of the estate that she was wont to accuse him of caring more for Upton than he did for herself.

Naturally, this argument always reached a most satisfactory conclusion, and despite all her protestations, she knew the day she was able to place his son in his arms would be as happy for her as it would be for him. She might tease him by declaring that she hoped the coming child would be a daughter, and indeed that she might give him a whole row of daughters, but Edward was not deceived!

Feeling that her cousin's praise of the Duke of Vern and Wraxton Priory was somewhat overdone, Harriet tried to interrupt her, but it was to no avail.

Before too long, Harriet had been regaled at great length by a breathless dissertation on the Duke's gallantry, the size of his undoubtedly vast estates, and his undeniable attractions as a husband for some fortunate young lady.

Happily for cousinly unity, Harriet was too deeply engrossed in her own thoughts to notice the emphasis which Sophy placed on this last statement. There was a rather considering gleam in the blue eyes as they regarded Harriet's aloof profile.

Jumping off the bed, Sophy all but dragged Harriet into her own bedchamber, throwing open the doors of a closet bursting with gowns. Pulling one out, she held it over her arm, telling her cousin that she had purchased it in a fit of madness before realizing that it would never suit her own coloring.

It was made of Nile green silk, as fine as a piece of gossamer, embroidered with crystals like teardrops that shimmered at the slightest movement. Harriet could not prevent herself from touching the delicate fabric.

"Take it," Sophy pressed. "I shall never wear it, and it might have been made for you!"

Indeed it might. It fitted Harriet perfectly, so perfectly that Harriet felt bound to bestow an old-fashioned look upon her cousin. She well knew that whereas she had lost weight since her return from London, Sophy had become prettily plump, but she had no wish to spoil the other's pleasure in the gift, so she accepted Sophy's assertion that she was doing her a favor by removing it from her wardrobe and promised that she would wear it for the ball.

When Harriet asked incuriously about the arrangements for the ball, Sophy informed her with airy insouciance that all manner of persons had been invited, although because of the hazards of winter travelling they were not having a formal dinner beforehand, a statement that Harriet accepted with relief. She had no wish to endure the ordeal of a long-drawn-out meal, especially under the curious and sympathetic eyes of those who had known her in London. A light meal in her room would suffice, she assured Sophy, wondering a little at the patent relief in her cousin's eyes when she offered this information.

She was not given the opportunity to wonder for very long. No sooner had Sophy disappeared in a flutter of silk skirts than a maid came bustling in with water for her bath and a jar of scented crystals made in the stillroom from Upton's own roses. It smelled delicious, and Harriet lingered in the warm water for so long that she was still not quite ready when Philip tapped on the door to escort her downstairs.

She bent her head so that the maid could adjust the fillet of diamonds Sophy had insisted on lending her, claiming that they went with the gown. Certainly the jewels looked very attractive, glittering in her burnished ringlets. As she picked up her fan and gloves, the green gown shimmered softly beneath the candles. The last few months had taken away the last vestiges of childishness from the contours of her face, revealing the purity of her bone structure, the high cheekbones and small jaw, emphasizing the depth and color of her eyes, turning her from a girl to a woman. Faint shadows underlined the pensive quality of her smile, her eyes still hold-the elusiveness of remembered unhappiness. She was thinner and swayed gracefully at Philip's side as they descended the stairs. Sophy's hand crept into her husband's as she watched their progress from the hall. Edward returned its pressure, smiling reassuringly as their eyes met in mutual concern.

The ballroom had been decorated since Sophy's marriage, and now, all hung with Christmas decorations, presented a charming picture. White flowers were banked around the walls, and a large fire blazed cheerfully at one end of the vast room, while at the other end the musicians were taking their places, toasting their host and hostess in the wine set out for their consumption.

Harriet had waltzed with Philip, performed a set of country dances with Edward, and listened to Sir George comparing Edward's lands to his own, before Lord Burbridge approached her.

He smiled, proffering his arm, which Harriet took. "Will you forgive me if, instead of dancing, I spirit you away to Edward's library? I have his permission, and I promise you I will not keep you away from the festivities for very long."

Behind the kind smile, graveness lurked. Harriet's heart leaped in fear. Had Lord Burbridge somehow learned about the Comte? Was he going to ask Harriet to help him bring his one-time friend to justice? Her fingers trembled on Lord Burbridge's arm, but she made no demur when he led her out of the ballroom and across the hall to Edward's library.

It was a comfortable room and plainly made ready for their occupation, for a decanter and glasses were set out temptingly on a table before the fire; two deep leather chairs were pulled up to its warmth.

Declining a glass of wine, Harriet watched Lord Burbridge sip his. It struck her that he was not completely at ease. He cleared his throat a little uncomfortably, and his very nervousness increased her fear.

"Harriet, I want to talk to you about a young friend of mine. I'm sure your cousin will already have mentioned him?"

Harriet stared at him in bewilderment.

"Perhaps I should say that I am here to act as his representative," Lord Burbridge amended hurriedly. "Harriet, my child, if you will just spare him ten minutes of your time . . ."

What was Lord Burbridge talking about? To whom was she to give her time?

Lord Burbridge was walking to the door. He paused before opening it. "Treat him as gently as you can, my dear, for he has suffered dreadfully, and I think, if you will, you can heal the wounds he has sustained over the last few months."

Before Harriet could demand an explanation, Lord Burbridge was gone. Scarcely had the door closed behind him than it opened again. Harriet swung around, her cheeks on fire, her back very firmly to the door.

"Harriet?"

It was the voice she had yearned to hear all through so many empty weeks, but now she barely recognized it, charged as it was with uncertainty in the place of arrogance, rough entreaty in the place of laconic mockery.

She was trembling, clasping her hands before her, hardly daring to believe her ears.

"Comte?"

She stared into the dark shadows by the door, desperately searching for the belovedly familiar face, half convinced that she but perceived a mirage.

He came into the room, hesitantly, his eyes never leaving Harriet's face. He looked gaunt, less controlled than she remembered him, only the piercing clarity of his gaze unchanged. It was a gaze that would always demand the truth, Harriet thought intuitively, no matter how painful.

"I never imagined that you . . ." She swallowed nervously. "Surely it is not safe . . . surely you should leave the country. . . ."

Unaware that she was wringing her hands, her eyes beseeched him to be less careless of his safety.

"What would you say if I told you I had put off my departure so that I could beg you to come with me? Would you do that, Harriet? Would you desert your family, the life you have always known, to come to the arms of a spy, a man who would have betrayed your country?"

"Please . . . you must not say such things!" Harriet cried. "If anyone should overhear you! Oh, why did you come here, endangering yourself like this?"

She could not meet his eyes. Her heart was behaving in a most ridiculous fashion. Even while she was agonizing over his safety, joy was sweeping through her on a flood tide that destroyed the barriers of pride and convention.

"Well, Harriet?"

The tone of his voice commanded her to lift her head. Shyly she did so. The gray eyes were warm as they had once been before. She caught her breath in a ragged gasp.

"You should not have come," she began brokenly, only to be interrupted by his harsh, "Why, because there is no hope for me—is that what you are trying to tell me?"

There was such raw agony in his voice, such pain that she threw caution to the winds. This time it was she who moved first, flying toward him, reassurances tumbling from her lips.

His arms opened wide to receive her. They were a haven, a safe sheltering place from the storm, the only home she would ever want. She raised her head to tell him so, and knew he had read of her love in her eyes as he bent his own, murmuring foolish broken phrases, stemming her words with his kisses, kisses such as she had never known before.

They really were like wine, she thought dreamily as she clung to him, for nothing else could explain her state of euphoria.

"You will come with me, then?" he whispered urgently against her ear. "You will marry me?"

The tautness of his body told her the importance of her answer. It took no more than a few seconds to smile shyly and murmur an incoherent "Yes" against the soft coolness of his muslin shirt, but in those few seconds Harriet knew the power that was hers. It made her feel humble as she buried her head against the reassuring warmth of his chest.

"Yes," she repeated more firmly, "tonight, if you wish." A sudden thought struck her. "Lord Burbridge, does he know the truth? Has he guessed that you are a spy?"

Above her the Comte frowned, and Harriet's heart dropped. Was her happiness to be snatched from her, after all? Surely even Lord Burbridge would not let the Comte escape to France if he knew the truth about him, fond though he had been of him.

The Comte released her, leaving her shivering and uncertain without the protecting warmth of his arms.

"Harriet, I have not been honest with you," he said abruptly.

"Not been honest? You mean you don't love me, you don't really want me, it was all . . ."

"No, no, never that!" he said roughly, catching her in his arms. The fierceness of his kiss took her breath away. Desire flamed smokily in his eyes, and Harriet felt a corresponding surge of longing. He kissed her deeply, letting her see the full measure of his need for her, so that they were both trembling when he eventually released her.

"Never think that! If you only knew the torment I have endured these past weeks, longing for you, dreaming of you only to awake and find you but a figment of my imagination! A thousand times I tormented myself with the memory of how your skin felt to the touch, how your eyes would flash when you were angry. Your pride, and loyalty, your innocence . . ." His voice had dropped to a husky whisper. "Harriet, I have lied to you."

She waited, a dozen conflicting explanations tormenting her. He was married. He could not take her to France. He . . .

"I am not the Comte de la Valle," he said simply at last.

"N-n-n-not? You mean you invented a title for yourself to aid you in your spying?"

"No," he said patiently. "I mean I am not a Frenchman, I was not stealing secrets to sell to the French, and I have no need to flee the country!"

It was all very confusing, and instead of feeling deliriously happy, Harriet only wanted to burst into tears.

"Who are you, then?" she asked crossly. "Or am I never to know?"

"Oh, I think you will have to," the Comte said whimsically, "especially if you are to marry me. You have heard of the Duke of Vern?"

"Oh, yes indeed," Harriet retorted bitterly. "His virtues have been dinned into my ears, morning, noon, and night since my arrival. Why, what is he to you?"

For the first time, Harriet had the novel experience of seeing him decomposed.

"Harriet, I *am* Vern!"

She sat down before her legs betrayed her, her hands clenched in her lap, her face pale as milk.

"You mean it was all a silly game—all the time you . . . Oh, no!"

It was just too much. Tears filmed her eyes, and her voice wobbled perilously. She hunted frantically for her handkerchief and instead was forced to accept that proffered by the Comte—no, not the Comte, she told herself crossly, but His Grace, the Duke of Vern. "How foolish you must have thought me," she said bitterly when she had herself under control. "How stupid and naive."

"No, I didn't," the Duke said firmly. "If you must have the truth, I thought you quite adorable—pig-headed, stubborn, certainly, damned intrusive at times, and I swear you nearly gave me gray hairs with your complete disregard for your own safety—but I never thought you foolish, my love. Rather, I was the fool, for embroiling myself in such a mess. You will never know how many times I longed to confess, to see admiration in those big brown eyes, and not contempt."

"But you were the one who was contemptuous of me," Harriet said unsteadily. "You were quite odious to me, always threatening me, always . . ."

"Kissing you," suggested the Duke, smiling as she blushed. "And why do you suppose that was?"

"To punish me?" Harriet quavered.

"More, it was punishment for myself," he said softly, coming toward her. "Every time I touched those intoxicating lips I only longed for more. In fact," he groaned, taking her in his arms, "I find it is an appetite that grows with feeding, and it is already far too long since I last indulged myself."

Naturally, this piece of foolishness could not be allowed to pass unremarked. Harriet struggled to find the words to tell the Duke that she believed not a single one of the very flattering remarks he was whispering in her ear, but instead found herself obliged to submit to the fiery possession of his kiss.

Some considerable time later, seated at his side, Harriet composed herself to learn the full story.

"It began when I returned home from the Peninsula to take up my inheritance," Vern told her. "Lord Burbridge approached me to ask if I would help them discover who was stealing important papers from the Foreign Office. It did not take long for us to realize that Fiennes was the most likely culprit—his disaffection with our present monarchy is well known. He is a Catholic, robbed of his inheritance by the blood bath of Culloden—who shall blame him? However, suspicion was one thing, proof another, so we devised a neat, foolproof trap—at least we thought it was until a certain rebellious, determined young lady came on the scene!"

Harriet dimpled a smile at him. "Oh dear, did I cause you an awful lot of trouble?"

"You most certainly did," agreed the Duke with mock severity. "Poor Burbridge was at his wits' end when he discovered that you had penetated my disguise. He was all set to devise some excuse to send you back home until young Wyclyffe obligingly provided me with the lever I was looking for. My poor Harriet, I treated you very badly, didn't I?"

Now it was Harriet's turn to be severe. "You did!" she agreed. "Especially when I knew all along that you *were* the smuggler, but why were you on the Marsh?"

"We knew there was a spy ring operating in London, and we also suspected Lady Mary to be part of it. It was her job to trap foolish young men into confiding matters to her con-

233

cerning military plans and defenses for the South Coast in the event of an invasion, that sort of thing. By a stroke of luck, we managed to intercept a letter from France to Lady Mary telling her that they were sending someone to help her." The Duke looked into Harriet's absorbed face and smiled. "The rest was simple. I merely took the gentleman's place, that was why you saw me on the Marsh. I was waiting for the real spy to arrive so that he could be placed under lock and key in Folkstone jail out of harm's way."

"And your connection with the Bourbons?" Harriet asked.

"Ah, yes, that was a necessary refinement. I had to keep in close contact with Burbridge and avoid suspicion. How better than by pretending to be a member of Louis's entourage?"

"And Lady Mary never suspected?"

He shook his head. "No. After all, many *émigrés* are flocking to Bonaparte's banner—a lot of them see in him a savior both for France and for themselves. Naturally, when Fiennes learned from Mary, to whom he had sold his previous information, who I was, he lost no time in stealing the list Lord Burbridge had purposely left in his desk. It was for this reason that Fiennes was given the post as secretary to Lord Burbridge, and as we suspected, he was not able to refuse the bait."

"So why did I surprise *you* going through Lord Burbridge's desk?" Harriet asked, puzzled.

The Duke smiled impishly. "Ah, you see I was putting the list into the desk. I own that day you caught me off guard."

"And that day at your house? Your visitor?"

"Lord Burbridge," the Duke returned promptly. "Once you had confided to him your suspicions of me, he was anxious for the success of our plot. Since we could not be seen to talk privately, he had to seek me out where we would be undisturbed. Even so, it was a grave risk. If Fiennes or Lady Mary had guessed . . ." His face grew grave. Following his train of thought, Harriet shuddered. If Lady Mary had suspected that he had been deceiving her!

"Forget Lady Mary," he commanded softly. "She has no part in our lives. My own regret is that by enchanting young Wyclyffe she caused you pain. For that alone I cannot regret her death."

It removed the last shadow from Harriet's happiness—the unvoiced thought that somewhere in a corner of his mind he might have cherished a fondness for the woman who had been his mistress.

"Not so," he murmured, reading her thoughts. "You are too innocent to know of these things, my love, but a man must sometimes—"

Trembling fingers silenced him. "There is no need to say any more," Harriet whispered. "She is dead, may she rest in peace."

"You are a generous foe," murmured the Duke, "and a generous lover, I hope!"

Harriet blushed, and declaimed, "Com . . . Your Grace . . ."

"Charles," the Duke prompted softly in amusement. "That at least is my own, and I have longed to hear it on your lips."

"Charles . . ." Harriet repeated shyly, her

235

words lost as the Duke's lips claimed hers in a kiss of tender promise. Harriet's heart swelled with love, like a flower opening to the warmth of the sun after the hard frost of winter. They were one, indivisible and invincible, all misunderstanding and pain washed away in the sweet rapture of their joy.

"You will marry me soon," commanded the Duke, with a return of his old arrogance. "The master bedroom at Wraxton possesses a four-poster far too large for a single gentleman, and I have already spent too many lonely nights in it to contemplate any more with even the slightest degree of resignation. I shall be a possessive lover," he warned her, "and once you are truly mine, I shall never give you up!"

Harriet could find no fault with this masterful pronouncement. She lifted her face to the Duke's. . . .

Sophy, impatient of learning how matters were going forward in her husband's library, tiptoed into the hall and opened the door, peeping cautiously into the silent room. The sight that met her eyes reassured her that all was well, far more efficiently than any number of words. Harriet was locked fast in the Duke's arms; his dark head was bent over her cousin's ringlets. Both of them were plainly lost in a world of their own.

"They will be wed before the year is out, mark my words!" she prophesied on her return to the ballroom.

In the library the Duke was making very much the same comment, although as he told

Harriet, blushing adorably at the light in his eyes, that it was just as well that there were such things as special licenses, for after so many months apart, he doubted his ability to wait more than a handful of days to make her his own and sweep her off to the privacy of Wraxton!

ABOUT THE AUTHOR
Caroline Courtney

Caroline Courtney was born in India, the youngest daughter of a British Army Colonel stationed there in the troubled years after the First World War. Her first husband, a Royal Air Force pilot, was tragically killed in the closing stages of the Second World War. She later remarried and now lives with her second husband, a retired barrister, in a beautiful 17th century house in Cornwall. They have three children, two sons and a daughter, all of whom are now married, and four grandchildren.

On the rare occasions that Caroline Courtney takes time off from her writing, she enjoys gardening and listening to music, particularly opera. She is also an avid reader of romantic poetry and has an ever-growing collection of poems she has composed herself.

Caroline Courtney is destined to be one of this country's leading romantic novelists. She has written an enormous number of novels over the years—purely for pleasure—and has never before been interested in seeing them reach publication. However, at her family's insistence she has now relented, and Warner Books are proud to be issuing a selection in this uniform edition.